PENGUIN CRIME FICTION

BOHANNON'S BOOK

Joseph Hansen is the author of some twenty-five novels—including the celebrated mystery series featuring Dave Brandstetter—and is also a renowned short-story writer. He and his wife Jane live with a household of dogs and cats in southwest Los Angeles.

Bohannon's Book

Joseph Hansen

Bohannon's Book

Five Mysteries

PENGUIN BOOKS

PENGUIN BOOKS
Published by the Penguin Group
Viking Penguin, a division of Penguin Books USA Inc.,
40 West 23rd Street, New York, New York 10010 U.S.A.
Penguin Books Ltd, 27 Wrights Lane, London W8 5TZ, England
Penguin Books Australia Ltd, Ringwood, Victoria, Australia
Penguin Books Canada Ltd, 2801 John Street,
Markham, Ontario, Canada L3R 1B4
Penguin Books (N.Z.) Ltd, 182-190 Wairau Road,
Auckland 10, New Zealand

Penguin Books Ltd, Registered Offices:
Harmondsworth, Middlesex, England

First published in the United States of America by
The Countryman Press Inc. 1988
Published in Penguin Books 1989

1 3 5 7 9 10 8 6 4 2

These stories first appeared in the following publications, and are
reprinted with permission:

"The Tango Bear," *Ellery Queen's Mystery Magazine*,
December, 1984

"Snipe Hunt," *Ellery Queen's Mystery Magazine*, February, 1986

"Witch's Broom," *Alfred Hitchcock's Mystery Magazine*, December, 1986

"Merely Players," *Alfred Hitchcock's Mystery Magazine*, February, 1987

"Death of an Otter," *Alfred Hitchcock's Mystery Magazine*, October, 1987

"The Tango Bear" also appeared in book form in the collection
Brandstetter & Others, and "Snipe Hunt" in the anthology
Murder, California Style.

LIBRARY OF CONGRESS CATALOGING IN PUBLICATION DATA
Hansen, Joseph, 1923–
Bohannon's book: five mysteries/Joseph Hansen.
p.   cm.—(Penguin crime fiction)
Contents: The tango bear—Snipe hunt—Witch's broom—Merely players—Death
of an otter.
ISBN 0 14 01.2053 X
1. Detective and mystery stories, American.   I. Title.
[PS3558. 513B6   1989]
813'.54—dc20   89-31806

Printed in the United States of America

*To Eleanor Sullivan and Cathleen Jordan
the editors who got me started
writing these and keep me at it*

over the counter like a broken marionette. His

Contents

The Tango Bear

Stubbs used to do the cooking, but it had pained Hack Bohannon to watch him. Stubbs had been a rodeo rider in his time. Young, being sent flying from the backs of sunfishing broncos hadn't stopped him. Tramplings and tossings by brahma bulls were all in a dusty day's work—or play. But he had broken a lot of bones, some of them more than once. And time is on no man's side. By forty, he was no longer fit for the rodeo circuit. And he had left forty far behind him when he came to look after Bohannon's stables up Rodd canyon, above Madrone. He could still ride like part of the horse, if he could get into the saddle. But walking was another matter. After a few months, Bohannon had taken over the cooking.

He didn't mind. It was a way to get the day started. It gave point to getting out of bed. More than a year ago, now, Linda was taken hostage on a rotten tub of a fishing boat full of brown Mexican heroin, beaten, raped, half-drowned, and broken in her mind so that she no longer knew him or anyone else. At the time, Bohannon had loaded the Winchester to shoot himself. But he couldn't do it. If your stupidity brought harm to someone you loved, you lived with that. He went to bed sober, though he knew his dreams would likely be terrible. And he rose in the morning, though he knew the day would be little better. Having to cook helped.

A lean, dark man, shaggy-haired, an inch over six feet, and lately turned forty himself, he stood at a window of the pine-plank kitchen, smoking, gazing out at the morning. The air that came in at the window was fresh, but the sky had a yellow tinge to it above the canyon trees and brush, which meant the day would be hot. And dry. When the hell was it going to rain? California canyons had a way of burning out. That was commoner down south. Here on the central coast, rains drifted in off the sea and regularly damped things down. In sheltered coves of these mountains, moss hung from the oaks. But this year, rain was scarce. Bohannon dreaded a fire. He stabled a lot of horses—other peoples' horses, but he cared about them all, beautiful, ugly, gentle, mean. Big as they were, they were helpless. And horses were fools in fire.

The kettle shrieked, and he crossed from the window to pour boiling water into a big blue enamel coffee pot. He filled the kettle, set it back on the burner, and was folding biscuit dough, gazing up at one of Stubbs's horse drawings on the wall, when the old man's worn boot heels thumped the plank walkway that fronted the ranch house. The door banged open. Stubbs was in a shaving phase. Damp made his knuckles hurt, and in rain and fog he let his white whiskers sprout. But this morning, his jowls were smooth and pink. His eyes were a blue that must have wowed the girls in the old days. Now they were round with surprise and worry.

"You better come with me," he said.

"Don't tell me it's Lewis's colt again." Bohannon sighed and rinsed the sticky dough off his hands. "I ought to charge them double for the nuisance." He pulled a shirt from a chairback and flapped into it. "What's he done this time?"

"It's no colt," Stubbs said. "It's a filly. She's pretty bunged up, too. Don't know how she got here, condition she's in." He hobbled away. Bohannon followed. "I never heard her. Rivera ought to heard her, but you know him. He sleeps the sleep of the blessed."

"What are you talking about?" Bohannon said.

"There's a girl in the empty box stall," Stubbs said.

There was. She lay asleep on fresh straw. Slender, young, about twenty, in jeans, blouse, fake suede zipper boots, floppy jacket—the kind of outfit girls at the college in Madrone wore. The clothes were torn and soiled. The girl's long, soft, dark hair had twigs and dry leaves tangled in it. Bohannon didn't like the way she was sleeping. He knelt and felt for a pulse. It was there, strong and regular. He saw blood on her other sleeve. He touched that sleeve and she gave a cry, opened her eyes, and cringed away from him.

"It's all right," he said. "We won't hurt you."

"Oh, God," she said, and pushed hair off her face. "I wanted to be gone by sunrise. I just couldn't walk any farther. I had to sleep." She tried to get to her feet, but the effort made her gasp. She went white and dropped to her knees. She put her good hand against the rough plank wall, planted a foot and tried to rise again. "I'll go on, now. I'm sorry for trespassing." The arm in the bloody sleeve

3

hung limp. She managed a brief smile. "Could you"—her eyes begged—"just not tell anybody I was here?"

"You're hurt bad," Stubbs said. "Who done it to you?"

"I had an accident," she said. "Drove off the road."

He doubted it, but Bohannon was grateful for every word she spoke. When he'd found Linda this way, torn, bruised, bloody, aboard that filthy boat, she wouldn't speak a word. She would never speak again. She had gone to hide inside herself forever. "There's a phone in the house," he said. "We can call the sheriff. Here, let me help you."

"No. Please, not the sheriff."

"Come on." Bohannon reached for her. But she twisted half away and his hand struck the dangling arm. She gave a sharp cry, fell face forward in the straw, and lay still.

"Fainted," Stubbs said. "That arm looks broke."

Bohannon picked her up and carried her into the house.

Belle Hesseltine said, "I think you're making a mistake." She shut the hall door behind her, set her medical kit on a chair beside that door, and came to the long deal table where Stubbs, Rivera, and Bohannon were eating.

Bohannon, mouth full, nodded, reached, dragged out a chair for her to sit on. She said, "You're borrowing trouble again. When are you going to learn?"

Bohannon swallowed and said, "Sit down. Try

the eggs. They've got tomatoes and jalepeños in them. Those are sourdough biscuits. *Hecho a mano.* From scratch." With a smiling shake of her head for Bohannon's willfulness, the doctor sat. Bohannon said, "You know Stubbs. Rivera?"

Rivera was young, fragile looking, a seminarian aiming at the priesthood. But he worked hard, was good with the horses, and stronger than he looked. He gave the doctor a shy smile. Women frightened him. Stubbs ducked his head. "Ma'am," he said. Doctors frightened him.

"She's terrified," Belle Hesseltine told Bohannon. "She's in some kind of trouble, and it's far more serious than a few bruises and contusions." She flapped open a napkin and laid it in her lap. "Even than a broken arm."

"You don't know her? Never saw her before?"

"There are fifteen hundred students on that campus." Belle Hesseltine spooned eggs onto her plate, speared sausage links, took a biscuit from the basket. "And most of them are healthy the year around. No, I don't know her."

"No identification on her," Stubbs said. "Maybe she ain't a student. Maybe she don't come from around here."

"That jacket was bought at a shop in Madrone," Bohannon said. "It's on the label. The boots are from San Luis. She's from around here someplace." He gulped the last of his coffee, laid the napkin beside his plate, pushed back his chair. "She claims she drove off the road. If I find the car, it could tell me who she is." He got to his feet.

"She's lying about that," Belle Hesseltine said. "There is no car. Her injuries aren't that kind. I've

5

treated a great many scrapes and bangs like hers. Those are hikers' injuries. She got those in a long, rough fall."

"People don't hike in the dark," Bohannon said.

"If it was only an accident"—Stubbs tilted back his chair and made a ragged cigarette—"what's she so scared of? Won't tell us her name. Don't want us to find her folks. We mustn't call the law. Didn't even want us to call you. Just says, let her hide here till she's better. I guess she didn't fall. I guess somebody pushed her."

"I guess so," Bohannon said. "I want to know why. Before she gets better. I want to know who."

"Be careful, Hack," Belle Hesseltine said. "She seems a lovely, well-bred girl, but appearances can be so deceiving. You don't know what she's into, and who's in it with her. Drugs, prostitution? Let the sheriff handle it."

Bohannon's laugh was sour. "If I hadn't let the sheriff in on that Mexican heroin smuggling case, Linda might still be here." He bent and kissed the doctor's soft, old cheek. "Thanks for the house call, Belle. And for keeping quiet about it."

"It's against my better judgment," she said strictly.

"I'll poke around, see what I can find." Bohannon went to the outer door. "I'll backtrack from the stables."

"It shouldn't take you long." The doctor rose abruptly from the table, making a face. Stubbs had lighted his cigarette. She waved away the smoke with a hand. "One of her ankles is badly sprained. She can't have come far." She gave Stubbs a severe

6

look. "You're old enough to have better sense. Tobacco will kill you."

"I've been run over by a herd of buffalo," Stubbs said. "If that didn't kill me, I can stand a little smoke."

Bohannon went out into the bright sunlight.

She had come from farther than anyone with a sprained ankle should have been able to. Fear could sometimes mask out pain. He was winded and wet with sweat by the time he had climbed out of a ravine of big old oaks to this ragged blacktop road. Gazing around at the brown slopes and ridges, he did some mental mapwork. After rolling and ricocheting down this hundred foot drop, she'd blundered through the dark a good five miles. The drop here was steep. He'd had to haul himself up by grabbing chaparral and rock, his clothes were torn now like hers, his hands bleeding the same way.

He stood, panting, looking up and down the road. A few yards along, black streaks of fresh rubber lay on the pitted asphalt that sun and rain had bleached to gray. Somebody had stopped a car there. He walked down for a closer look. That car had been going far too fast for such a twisting road. It had also stopped too fast, skidded a long way, swerving wildly, damn near out of control. He gauged it was a big car, heavy, the tires new.

In the morning stillness, the sound reached him now of another car coming. He stepped onto the road shoulder. The car came around a bluff where a gnarled pine leaned out above the road. The car was taking its time. It wasn't a car he recognized—beige, two-three years old, compact, anonymous. He didn't recognize the driver, either. Ranch hat with a curled-up brim, little neckerchief, open collar, whipcord jacket, everything tan. Bohannon gave him a neighborly nod and lift of the hand. The man drove past. If he saw Bohannon it was from behind wrap-around sunglasses. He probably didn't see Bohannon. He was looking at the landscape. The landscape here was worth looking at.

Bohannon stepped into the road and crouched. Between last night's skidmarks, where they ended, lay a spot of oil. Fresh, no dust on it. He chewed his lower lip. Funny. The car must have stood here for a time. What the hell for? He straightened, knees giving small cracks that said he was too old for this, and walked back along the road. Dry brush edged the blacktop, knee-high. Many yards back, just about even with the place where the tire tracks began, right at the spot where Bohannon judged the girl had tumbled into the ravine, the brush was smashed flat. He knelt and examined it. A swatch of calico caught his eye—the fabric of the girl's shirt. He unsnagged it and pushed it into a pocket with the other bits he'd found along her trail, a drawstring from her jacket, a decorative bootstrap.

Out of the pocket he drew a V-shaped rag of tweed. He blinked at it in his fingers. He lifted his eyes and looked back along the road to where the car had stopped and unaccountably waited. The girl had worn no tweed, but Bohannon had found this caught on a fallen oak branch down below. So, had the driver of the car worn tweed, left the car, clambered down after her? It looked like it. Why? Had he tried to kill her by pushing her out of the car as it tore along through the night? Had he left the car and followed to make sure she was really dead? Or had she jumped from the car, and had he followed to fetch her back? He'd failed. Her fear had outrun his purpose, whatever it was. Bohannon frowned at the scrap, fingered it. Good tweed, hand-loomed. Expensive. He gave his head a shake, pushed the bit of wool back into his pocket, and headed for home, wishing for a horse.

When he got back to the place, kids on horses came swaying out the gate, saddle leather creaking. Stubbs helped two small children ride slowly around the paddock. A young couple from Los Osos wanted boarding and exercise rates—they were leaving on a cruise. In the shadows of the stable, Rivera helped the blacksmith from over in Paso Robles. It seemed an ordinary day. As Bohannon showered, he saw out the bathroom window horses grazing the long pastures that sloped up to the sunburned mountains, horses standing sleepily together in the shadows of oaks. A peaceful scene. What was a frightened girl doing in the middle of it?

While he heated soup for her, he built her a thick beef and cheese sandwich, and poured a glass of milk. Carrying bowl, sandwich, milk on a tray, he rapped the door of the room where they'd put her. She made a sleepy sound that he took to be permission to enter. She moved drowsily under a patchwork quilt on an old pine poster bed. Blinking, trying to smile, pushing hair off her face, which was badly scraped down one side, she sat up. The broken arm was in a neat sling. Bohannon set the tray on the bedside table, and arranged pillows for her so she could manage the tray on her lap.

"I'll repay you for all this," she said solemnly.

"All right." He dragged a chair to the bedside, sat down, put his hands on his knees, and told her what he had done with his morning. "After you jumped out of the car, he stopped it and tried to follow you. It was too dark, and he gave up. But only for the time being—right?"

She ate with the hunger of the healthy young, spooning up the thick, home-made soup. She gave him a quick glance. "This is good. Thank you. I was starving. But I won't stay and eat you out of house and home. I'll be on my way, now."

"Not on that ankle. On your way where?"

"It's not your worry." She took a big bite of the sandwich, chewed a while, washed the bite down with a long gulp of milk. "Someplace far away."

"You didn't bring any money," he said.

"I'll be all right. You've done all you could." She finished off the soup. "Lucky for me I stumbled on your place. There aren't that many kind people left in the world."

"That sounds grownup," Bohannon said, "but not calling the law when someone's trying to kill you—that doesn't."

"Kill me?" She opened her eyes wide, mocking him.

"Rape you, then," Bohannon said.

She stared. Color crept into her face. "What?" Her laugh was brief and sad. "Rape? Oh, no." She frowned. "You ask questions like a policeman." She looked out the window. "But you're not. You're a rancher. Horses."

"I was a deputy sheriff for fourteen years," he said. "Just about long enough to learn that people only jump from speeding vehicles for very serious reasons."

She bit her lip to keep from smiling. Her eyes never smiled. "He won't find me here."

"He knows the kind of fall you had, knows you had to be hurt and couldn't go far. There's a seminary over that ridge." He lifted an arm to point. "There's Ludlow's apple ranch down Sills canyon. And there's here. Not many places to have to search. And he's searching, isn't he?"

"I said I'd go." She glared at him, picked up the tray, pushed it into his hands. "Thank you for the meal. And for the doctor. And the wash and the sleep. But I don't want to put you in any danger." She flung back the bedclothes. Belle had put her into an old pair of his pajamas, cuffs rolled up on the pants and one sleeve, the other sleeve hanging because of the sling. She swung her legs over the bedside and tried to stand. "Oh, wow," she whispered, and went white, and sat down hard.

"I'm not in any danger." Bohannon set the tray on the floor and helped her lie back against the pillows again. He pulled the quilt up over her. "But you are. Tell me his name, and what this is all about. I can help you."

She lay with her eyes shut. She shook her head. "No. That's where you're wrong. You're sweet, but you're wrong." She opened her eyes. She was very earnest. "There are things that happen to us that no one can help us with. It's a big world, with billions of people in it, but some of them are all alone, and always will be." She closed her eyes again, and two tears ran down her face.

"I don't understand," Bohannon said. "The man terrifies you, yet you're protecting him."

"You do understand," she said, and was asleep.

Bohannon picked up the tray and softly left the room.

What kind of magazines would she like? The rack in the cool arcade of boutiques off the sunny main street in San Luis appeared to have every kind there was. She didn't seem to him the *Good Housekeeping* sort. He chose the *New Yorker, Los Angeles,* and one called *Ms.* Television reception was bad at his place because of the surrounding mountains, and cable hadn't come in yet. Reading would help her pass the time.

Magazines under his arm, he went along the shadowy corridor to a lively high-countered place that made fancy sandwiches and had Anchor steam beer on draft. It was great beer. He carried a tall cold glass of it out into the sunshine and sat by a rocky stream there to drink it among noisy college youngsters. He smoked cigarettes and let time slide because he hated going to the sheriff's station.

But after a second beer, he made himself go. A good many men in sand-color uniforms spoke his name in the halls, and he spoke theirs. But he felt more out of place here now than any stranger. He ended up in an office that had once been his—before he had resigned over the whitewash of an officer who in cold blood had shot down an unarmed Latino kid. Gerard sat at a desk still piled with too much work for one man to handle.

Gerard didn't smile at Bohannon, and Bohannon would never in his life again smile at Gerard. But Gerard got Bohannon the missing person file without comment, without question. He knew better than to ask Bohannon to sit down, and Bohannon remained standing to leaf through the file. People kept wandering off, but none of them on any of these sheets remotely resembled the sad, frightened girl in his spare bedroom. He handed the file back with thanks, and walked out of the station as quickly as he could. To him, it smelled of death.

The attendance office of the sprawling new Madrone Community College smelled only of fresh paint. But the woman in charge simply smiled disbelief when Bohannon asked about absent female students, and passed over the counter to her a drawing of the girl he'd had Stubbs make from memory. Stubbs was best at horses, but he could draw a good human likeness when he put his mind to it and his knuckles didn't hurt too much. The woman set reading glasses on her beaky nose, examined the drawing, handed it back. She pulled the glasses down and looked at him over them. "I'm sorry. She might be almost anyone." Bohannon had to agree. Crossing the campus to get here, he had passed at least a dozen.

He drove north from the college toward the town, a clutch of spindly Victorian frame houses on sleepy, narrow streets. Behind it, livestock grazed foothills. Farther back, the mountains rose. To the west, the pine-forested hills of Settlers Cove blocked out sight of the ocean, scarcely a mile away. The town was trying to wake up. Fresh paint had been laid on the jigsaw work and turrets of the old houses—wedding cake tints. On the main street, shopfronts had been rusticated with planks to look like a set decorator's notion of the Olde West. He didn't care for that. Tourists were supposed to. So far, not many had—dogs still slept in the middle of the main street. Bohannon only came here for the shop that sold coffee beans.

Outside town, in a meadow with a little stand of pines at the lower end, where rumor had it a new shopping center was going to be built someday soon, he was surprised to find tents pitched, a Ferris wheel and other shiny rides set up, a faded canvas midway with games of chance and hot dog stands—a traveling carnival. Metallic music reached him in the pickup as he passed. He saw loudspeaker horns on tall barber-striped poles that held strings of lightbulbs and plastic pennons, red, blue, yellow, green, that fluttered in the wind. He shook his head. He couldn't recall a carnival ever stopping in Madrone before. He drove on to the coffee bean place.

The sun was setting behind his own hills when he got back to the stables and ranch house in Rodd canyon, braked the pickup in a swirl of dust, and climbed down out of it with the magazines and sacks of coffee beans. He slammed the tinny cab door and made for the kitchen, where Stubbs was at the stove, pushing food around in a big skillet.

The old man had a clock in his head. Things had to happen on time. It was good for the business—horses thought the same way. Supper time was supper time. Bohannon set down his burden and went to the stove for a look. Stubbs glanced at him. "Turkey hash. All right with you?"

"Smells good," Bohannon said.

"You know a fella named Williams?" Stubbs asked.

"No. What about him?" Bohannon found a tumbler in a cupboard, ice cubes in a lumbering old refrigerator. "Did he come here? What for?"

"Said he'd like to buy your spread." Stubbs salted the hash from a big tin shaker. "He looked the stables over, nail by nail. Squinted into every corner. Not too easy for him, either. Walks with them aluminum crutches that clamp around your arms. Short legs, all bent out of shape. Worse off than me."

Bohannon took the glass of ice and a bottle of Old Crow to the table. The table was neatly set. As always when Stubbs cooked, a big jug of ketchup stood in the middle. Bohannon sat down and poured himself a drink. "It's not for sale. Why did you let him waste his time?"

"He don't know the meaning of 'not for sale'."

Bohannon tasted the whiskey and lit a cigarette. "You been keeping an eye on the girl? Did you ask her if she likes turkey hash?"

"She's mostly been asleep," Stubbs said. "Them painkillers do that to you. Found her once, trying to get to the bathroom. That's a mighty tender ankle. I expect she's sore pretty much all over. Way I remember it. Be worse tomorrow. Poor little thing. I carried her to and fro."

"Keep that up," Bohannon said, "and you'll be down in bed, yourself."

"Williams wanted to look through the house," Stubbs said. "I told him he'd have to ask you. Acted like he didn't hear. Headed straight for it, hauled himself up on the porch, started peeking in the windows."

"It was a beige compact, right?" Bohannon said. "He wore wrap-around sunglasses, a little neckerchief, cowboy hat with the brim crimped up on the sides?"

"You do know him," Stubbs said.

"He doesn't want to buy this place," Bohannon said. "He's looking for the girl. I saw him this morning."

"I run him off." Stubbs limped to the kitchen door, pushed open the screen, leaned out, and whistled for Rivera. He let the screen fall shut and frowned at Bohannon. "You think he's the one that tried to kill her?"

"And so do you," Bohannon said. "You didn't say anything to her about him, I hope."

Stubbs shook his head. "I'm smarter than I look. I figured she'd try to run away, and she ain't ready for that." He rattled plates down out of a cupboard. "I thought you said it was a heavy car."

"A man can change cars." Bohannon worked on his drink. "Did you get the license number?"

"Covered with mud," Stubbs said. "Neat. Like it was laid on with a paintbrush. And I don't see like I used to."

"Probably a rental car," Bohannon said, "and if

we checked, it wouldn't be any Williams anybody ever knew."

Rivera came in with his hair slicked down by water.

Bohannon awoke in pitch darkness. That was wrong. Ground lights glowed outside all night. Up in the meadow, horses were running hard, nickering, afraid. In the stables, horses snorted fear, hoofs kicked walls. Bohannon left the bed so fast he fell. He groped for the Winchester by the dresser where it always stood. But tonight Rivera had it. Bohannon had posted him on a kitchen chair on the porch outside the girl's room to guard her. Bohannon poked into a shirt, yanked on pants, leaned out the window. "Rivera?" He couldn't see. He tried the lightswitch. No light. A power outage? They were common enough in storms, but tonight was calm and clear. "Rivera?" Bohannon climbed out the window onto the porch. He could hear Stubbs cussing out the horses in the stables. Bohannon didn't head that way. He ran along the planks to the girl's room. The chair was there—he stumbled over it. But the man he fell against was not Rivera. This was a thick man with a bad smell to him.

"What's the matter?" It was the girl's voice, thin.

"Stay down," Bohannon shouted. The man struggled. Bohannon got a knee in the mouth. He tried for a better grip, and the man twisted away from him. Bohannon, on hands and knees, saw the man above him, silhouetted against faint starlight. The man raised the rifle and swung it down.

Bohannon ducked, but the stock struck his shoulder, and he heard bone crack. He lay on his face and for a moment knew only pain, no sight, no sound, no thought. Then he heard the man running away. Groaning, Bohannon struggled to his feet. He clutched a porch post. "Catch him, Rivera," he shouted. "Catch him, Stubbs." He reeled off the porch and tried to run.

The girl called from the window. "What is it?"

"Horse thief," Bohannon lied. "Happens all the time." The motor of a large vehicle thrashed to life out in the road. Headlights went on out there. Gears clashed, a hulking, dark shape lurched down the trail. Shaggy eucalyptus trees edged the property there. He couldn't see well, but damned if the thing didn't look like a horse van. He opened his mouth to shout at it, but no sound came. He collapsed in the dust.

He awoke in his bed with his arm bound tight across his ribs, and sun pouring in the window. Stubbs stood beside the bed with a tray of food. He grinned. "Belle Hesseltine says if you mixed that shot she give you with whiskey you'd sleep forever." Bohannon numbly blinked and yawned. The memory came back vaguely of gaunt, grim Belle, by the soft light of a kerosene lamp, setting his collar bone at three in the morning, and saying sternly, "I told you so, and I'm not ashamed to say it. Now, you put that girl in the sheriff's hands. That man could have shot you dead."

Bohannon had said, "He didn't come to shoot."

"Can you sit up?" Stubbs said. "You want help?"

Bohannon shook his head, pushed himself into position with his right arm. "What time is it?"

"Noon." Stubbs set the tray on Bohannon's knees. "Been all quiet and regular so far." He sat down. "Them's poached eggs. Invalid food."

"Did the girl believe me about the horse thief?"

"I looked in twice. All she does is sleep."

"Good." Bohannon ate for a moment in silence, frowning. He blinked at Stubbs. "What upset the horses? They don't pay any attention to the lights going out."

"Not as a rule," Stubbs said. "Power company come and fixed the line an hour ago. Cut, all right. Deliberate."

"He meant to take the girl," Bohannon said.

"So it was smart to stir up the horses," Stubbs said. "Rivera run off to see what was bothering them. He's ashamed of himself, feels like he let you down bad. Specially about the rifle—leaving the rifle behind for that bastard."

Bohannon made to shrug and felt pain. "Rivera didn't want the rifle from the start. Priests don't shoot people. It was natural for him to forget it."

"I didn't take the horses acting up for what it was." Stubbs shook his head sadly. "A diversion. If I'd of had my wits about me, I'd have come direct to help the girl."

"You did right." Bohannon drank coffee. Stubbs had ground some of the new beans. The coffee was fine. "But I still don't know what got into them." He pointed. "You want to light me a cigarette, please? They're in my shirt."

Stubbs got cigarette pack and matches from the shirt, lit a cigarette and gave it to Bohannon, wrinkled his nose, turned back, picked up the shirt and smelled it. "Well, I'll be," he said mildly. "Bear." He dropped the shirt.

Bohannon stared at him through smoke. "Bear?"

"That's what scared the horses," Stubbs said. "Never thought I'd get a whiff of bear again. Last time was in Wyoming, nineteen and twenty eight. I was working cattle for a fella by the name of—"

"It was on his clothes," Bohannon said. "Rank. I remember wondering how any man could smell like that."

"Beats me," Stubbs said. "You and me smell like horse a lot of the time, but we live with horses. Nobody lives with a bear."

"The carnival," Bohannon said.

But he didn't go there. Dressed, a little stupified by the drug Belle had shot him full of, but able to navigate on his feet and ready to drive the pickup, he was halfway to it, jingling the keys, when he remembered what Stubbs had said about the girl. He went back inside, rapped her door, waited, opened the door. A shape was under the patchwork quilt, all right. But it wasn't her shape. He knew it before he threw the quilt back. She had laid pillows underneath.

Her boots had stood on the shiny broad floorboards beside the chest of drawers. They were gone. Stubbs had washed her clothes and laid them in a drawer. He pulled the drawer open. Nothing. He left the room, wondering how much of a head start she had on him. Only one answer made sense. She had left as soon as she could after the man had left—the man who smelled like a bear. She had fled in panic. He couldn't blame her. But chancy as his protection had proved, she was worse off on her own. He had to bring her back.

He chose a gray gelding called Seashell. He wouldn't shy at a clumsy mounting, and he was sure-footed, and Bohannon believed the girl would keep away from roads and not seek a place full of people this time. He'd have to look for her where there weren't always trails. Watching Rivera saddle the gray, Bohannon disliked himself for wishing the girl pain. But he hoped that ankle was making travel slow for her. He hoped Stubbs's memory of how her kind of bruises felt two days afterward was right. Rivera held Seashell's head while Bohannon used a child's mounting block to crawl awkwardly into the saddle.

"Don't get down," Rivera said. "You can't get back up."

Bohannon found her trail nearby, but soon lost it. He crossed and recrossed ridges, firebreaks, circled clumps of oak, waded through chaparral, traced barrancas, most of them dry, one with a little trickle of a creek rambling down it. And here was a place where she had stopped to rest. She had knelt to drink from the creek. Her limp showed plainly in the indentations of her boots in the sand here. But she had left the sand before long. Lunging, Seashell got Bohannon up out of the barranca.

The sun was going down. He was in Sills canyon, and ready to give up. It was too far. He had missed her somehow back along the track. He was weary from the saddle, and the ache in his shoulder was strong. He wanted a drink, a hot bath, a meal, and

sleep. He reined the patient gray around, and headed homeward by a trail he hadn't taken. After a
mile or two, he sighted the burnt-out cabin. The
chimney stood, three walls, a section of roof. Burnt
out so long ago he couldn't recollect when. He
eased Seashell down there. And before he reached
the yard, he heard her weeping. Brush crackling under the horse's hoofs, Bohannon walked him close
and looked inside. She was huddled on the hearth.

"Aren't you hungry?" he said. "You didn't bring
food."

She nodded mutely, wiping her nose on her jacket sleeve, like a little kid. Sobs still jerked her when
she pushed up off the hearth and came forlornly
hopping through the trash, bottles, cans on the
floor. She held onto a charred upright and gazed at
him. He slid down from the horse—it was almost a
fall. He held out the reins to her.

"I never rode a horse," she said.

"I'll lead him, then," Bohannon said. "You just
sit in the saddle, all right? Come on, I'll help you
up."

"I can't sleep in that room again," she said.

"They won't be back," he said. "I'm going after
them."

She stared. "You don't know who they are."

"I know who one is," he said. "That's a start."

"I didn't tell you," she said. "Please remember
that."

The dusty bulbs strung on frayed and sagging
wires from the striped poles lit the tent tops now,
and made of the carnival an island of hectic bright-

ness in the night. The fast rides whirled, their gaudy red, blue, gold metal pods gleaming and glinting, children hanging on white-knuckled, trailing shrieks of joy and terror. The Ferris wheel rose sedate against the stars, the wheel strung with tiny lights that were like stars themselves, the seats of the wheel swinging grandmotherly as rocking chairs. The faces of the riders were pale ovals in the fairy tale glow.

He climbed stiffly down from the pickup onto the trampled grass of the meadow, among disorderly rows of newer pickups, campers, family cars, and heard the wheeze of an orgatron, the thin clash of its cymbals, the rattle of its snare drum. Walking past the noisy, hulking generator trucks, he smiled when he sighted a miniature merry-go-round, all carved and gilded and aglitter with mirrors, the small horses all curly manes and tails and flared nostrils, rising and sinking on their shiny poles, carrying cowboys three, four, five years old, wide-eyed with wonder.

The midway was crowded with high school and college youngsters, loud and rollicking, munching tacos and hotdogs, guzzling soft drinks from cans. Some of them tried hard to look superior and bored—a carnival was corny, after all, strictly hicktown. But Bohannon judged most of them had never had a crack at one before, and would remember it forever, no matter what they pretended. The canvas caves of yellow light that held the baseball throws, the rifle shoots, the wheel of fortune were doing business just as brisk as the one where a battery of new electronic games beeped and twittered.

At the end of the midway—it wasn't a long

walk—the circular show tent loomed up behind a limp facade of weathered canvas posters. The smell of animals was strong here on the cool night air, the smells of tanbark and Cracker Jacks. Bohannon looked at the faded paintings of llamas, zebras, seals. Trick dogs wore tiny clown hats and tutus. Young men in white hung upside down from trapezes. A pretty young lady walked a tightwire. Two young blacks on tall unicycles played basketball. And here was what he had come for. THE TANGO BEAR. The sign painter had made the bear about ten feet tall and snarling. *See him dance. See him rollerskate. See him ride a motorcycle.*

The window of the truck from which tickets were sold was closed. Bohannon knocked on it. No one opened it. He made his way around to the back of the tent. A good many of what you might mistake for horse vans stood here in the near darkness. Their doors hung open, though. The animals were behind the canvas at his back. He could hear them shift and breathe and munch. A hoof clattered a bucket. Bohannon dropped to his knees and lifted the tent flap to peer inside. He wasn't looking for hoofs, flippers, paws. He hoped to see human feet. And he did—in manure-crusted work shoes.

A freckled, red-haired girl in dirty jeans and flannel shirt too big for her, the tails almost to her knees, looked down at him. "Aren't you a little old for sneaking in?" She had the voice of a very tough small boy. "Buy a ticket."

"Nobody will sell me one." Bohannon worked himself under the canvas, gripped a pole, pulled himself to his feet. A fat zebra kicked backward at him. He jumped aside. "Where do I find the Tango Bear?"

"Last sighted parked up by Hearst Beach," she said. "He missed both daytime shows. If he doesn't get back here"—she glanced at a wristwatch—"in twenty-five minutes, Mr. Cathcart will probably kill him. Not the bear. Pancho, I mean. What is it about Pancho?" The girl regarded Bohannon's bad arm. "Only cripples want to see him."

"You mean Williams? Aluminum crutches?"

"That's the one." A taffy-colored llama nosed the girl's butt. She gave its muzzle a slap. "Gertrude, I told you, no more carrots." But Gertrude was not taking no for an answer, and the girl moved her pockets out of the llama's reach. "Williams scares Pancho. Are you going to scare him too?"

"He borrowed something of mine last night," Bohannon said. "I'd like to have it back. I'll be around for a while. Don't tell him I'm looking for him." He offered her a twenty-dollar bill. She shook her head. He put the money away. "I want it to be a surprise," he said.

"Williams is coming tonight," she said. "That's why I told Mr. Cathcart not to worry about Pancho turning up for the evening show. Pancho won't cross Williams."

"You're a psychologist," Bohannon said.

She shrugged. "I live with animals." She reached into the loose shirt and brought out a tiny monkey. It scampered up her arm to perch on her shoulder, lean against her ear, peer anxiously at Bohannon, and squeak. The girl said, "After while, you figure them out, and people are no different."

The fat zebra kicked at Bohannon again.

"Except meaner," the girl said.

Bohannon sat on the grass with his back against the vibrating wheel of one of the mobile generators. He was in shadow, and he could watch the highway from here. Laughter and shouts came from the midway, the rides. The merry-go-round music wheezed. Cars and pickups and RVs arrived and departed from the parking area. He watched for the beige compact. Maybe a large car, too, expensive. And he watched for the van that held the Tango Bear. A voice crackled through the trumpet-shaped metal loudspeakers up the poles.

"Hur-ry, hur-ry, hur-ry. The big show is about to begin in the main tent. Get your tick-ets now, folks." The voice was a rasp, the words a drone. "Thrills, spills, chills. Ac-ro-bats, clowns, wild animals, death defying trap-eze acts. Perform-ing poodles from Par-ee. Won-der-ful trained seals. See the two-ton Tango Bear. He'll dance for you. This isn't TV, folks. This is all real, hap-pen-ing live before your ve-ry eyes. Don't miss it. You'll never for-give yourself. The ticket office is now open at the end of the mid-way. Hur-ry, hur-ry, hur-ry. Get your tick-ets now . . . "

The background of the highway as he viewed it was thick pine wood climbing slopes. Dark. Out of the darkness loomed the van, and lumbered along toward the big tent. Bohannon rose and watched. Lettering showed up on the side of the truck as it came into the light. THE TANGO BEAR. Bohannon started for the midway. The voice blared on from the loudspeakers. "Hur-ry, hur-ry, hur-ry." He took the advice, pressing through the crowd, trying not to jar his sore shoulder, not always avoiding it. He wanted to reach Pancho before the man was joined by his two-ton, ten-foot-tall friend.

He jammed for a minute in the crowd around the ticket truck. He was told to watch who he was shoving, and was himself shoved. He tripped over a tent stake and sprawled. Pain from his shoulder immobilized him for a moment. Then he used a bristly guy rope to haul himself to his feet. And in that instant, he glimpsed Williams in a seersucker suit at the far end of the midway. He was hobbling toward Bohannon as fast as he could on his shiny crutches. Bohannon wanted to talk to him, but he'd better get to Pancho first. He jogged around the tent to where the animal vans stood in the dark.

The rear doors of the Tango Bear truck were not open like the rest. He banged on them. The bear grunted and shuffled inside. Bohannon looked into the cab of the van. No Pancho. A tent flap let out a triangle of light. He stepped inside. The freckle-faced girl was in spangled white costume now, a tiara in her red hair. She didn't look the same. Her fairy godmother had been here. Bohannon envied the prince. The girl had blanketed the llamas in red and blue velvet with rhinestones, and crowned the zebras with silver and black plumes. She blinked sparkly false eyelashes at Bohannon.

"I heard Pancho's truck," she said. "Where is he?"

"That's what I was going to ask you," Bohannon said.

"Go find him," she said, "and tell him to get in here."

"Maybe he's with Williams," Bohannon said, and went out into the dark.

But now he had lost Williams. Williams hadn't joined the friendly folk around the window of the ticket truck. Bohannon started up the midway, eyeing the dwindling crowd. Williams wasn't pitching baseballs, throwing darts, or buying chances on a number on the big wheel. He wasn't frowning in concentration at the controls of an electronic game, nor among the jumping kids at the high, hot, greasy counters of the food trucks. Bohannon cut around behind the rows of tents, striding along through shadow and light, squinting into the dark slots between the tents. Nothing on the west side. He tried the east, the merry-go-round music in his ears.

The rear window of a food truck slapped open, and a bucket was emptied just in front of him. The window slapped shut. He muttered and brushed at his splashed pants legs. He walked on—and saw movement between two booths, in a space scarcely wide enough for a man. Light from a pole glared down into his eyes. He shaded them with his hand. And saw a thickset man, back turned, crouching in the dark. Bohannon opened his mouth to call out and then said nothing. The man held a rifle. Light from the midway beyond him slid along its barrel. Bohannon caught the noise of a round being jacked into the chamber, and he knew the gun was his Winchester.

Bohannon eased himself between the canvas

walls and smelled the bear smell. He tried to make no sound, stepping with care in case there were objects to fall over. He kept his eyes on the man, until the man lifted the gun to his shoulder to aim it. Then Bohannon looked for the target. Across the bright midway, Williams stood, holding a burrito that leaked chili sauce onto its paper wrapper. He was talking to a slight man with a neatly trimmed gray beard, who looked out of place at a carnival. *Distinguished* would be the easy word for him. His attitude seemed urgent.

"Hold it, Pancho," Bohannon said. "Don't shoot."

Pancho glanced over his shoulder, panic in his eyes, then turned back and fired the rifle. Bohannon lunged at him and got him in a choke hold. But Pancho dug a thick elbow into Bohannon's bound arm, and pain shot through Bohannon's shoulder, and he fell back. Pancho scrambled over him, a boot scraping Bohannon's cheekbone, another boot kicking off from Bohannon's stomach. Gasping, sick, Bohannon staggered to his feet and lurched toward the rear of the slot. Light glared in his eyes again. He couldn't see Pancho. And this time he didn't hear him running off. A motorcycle engine spluttered to life. Its lights flicked on. Bohannon ran for it. But it jumped away, jouncing out of the light across the meadow, toward the dark highway.

See him ride a motorcycle. Not tonight.

There was turmoil around the burrito truck. The fat, brown woman who ran it wept loudly in Spanish. A skinny, blond youngster in a white coat hung over the counter like a broken marionette. His starchy little white cap lay trampled in the grass, and his blood dripped on it. Ambulance attendants climbed into the truck and got the boy out and onto a gurney, a blanket over him, plasma leaking into his arm from a plastic pouch. He was pale but breathing. Bohannon prayed the bullet had done him no mortal harm. The gurney slid with a clatter into the ambulance, the doors slammed, and together Bohannon and Gerard, in tan sheriff's uniform, watched the ambulance rock slowly off down the midway, its siren moaning softly to warn people out of its track.

"He was aiming," Bohannon said, "at a man named Williams." He described Williams to Gerard. "He should be easy to find."

"What's the connection?" Gerard said.

"I don't know. The girl who looks after the animals"—Bohannon pointed at the big tent—"you might ask her. She said Pancho was scared of Williams. Maybe she knows why."

"He stole your rifle last night," Gerard said. He was studying the way Bohannon's left arm was strapped across his middle, the way Bohannon's sleeve hung empty. "Did he shoot you with it first?"

"Used it for a club," Bohannon said. "If he'd shot, he would have hit somebody else, wouldn't he?"

"He's no marksman," Gerard admitted. "Why would he go clear up there to steal a rifle? Are you leveling with me?"

"It's what happened," Bohannon said. "He brought his van with the bear in it. Panicked my horses. He climbed the pole and cut off the electricity. Why? Ask him. That's not much of a motorcycle. He shouldn't be hard to catch up to."

From the big tent came the noise of a small band, bass drum, cymbals, sousaphone, a trumpet, a trombone, a piccolo. They were making a try at "The Entrance of the Gladiators," but it didn't sound as if they were going to finish together. Bohannon would have liked to see the show. Particularly the red-haired girl, whatever she did. But he was too tired. He said to Gerard:

"Can I go home now?"

"You should have reported the rifle stolen," Gerard said.

"Yeah, yeah," Bohannon said, and limped away.

It was another clear, dry morning. Everyone was at the pine table in the kitchen eating breakfast—the girl too. The sound of a car coming into the yard made her stand up and start hopping for the hall doorway. She had her plate in her hand and the fork on it rattled at every hop. Aching all over, Bohannon went to the kitchen door and looked out. The car was a sheriff's department vehicle and Gerard was already out of it and striding along the porch, the Winchester in his hands. When he saw Bohannon holding the screen door open, he lifted the rifle and asked, "This yours?"

"Yes. Come in." Bohannon stood aside. Gerard entered the kitchen and stopped, looking at the girl with her plate in one hand and the other arm in a sling. "My niece," Bohannon said. "Lieutenant Gerard." He let the screen door close.

Gerard nodded to the girl. "Like a hospital around here."

"She fell off a horse," Bohannon said. "Breakfast?"

"Coffee, if you can spare it." Gerard pulled out a chair at the table and sat down. He said to Stubbs and Rivera, "Gentlemen." He said to Bohannon, who brought the blue pot from the stove, "He wasn't hard to catch, because he stopped."

Bohannon poured coffee, and glanced at the girl. He wanted her out of the room, and he jerked his head. The problem was she couldn't open the door with the plate in her hand. He set the pot down, opened the door for her, shut it after her, came back to the table. He asked Gerard, "What did he tell you?"

"Nothing. He's dead. Left the motorcycle on the road shoulder and jumped off a two-hundred-foot cliff. Maybe he meant to hit the ocean. He hit the rocks. You know the place. Bull sea lions loaf around down there, bellowing. There's a good echo." Gerard dug in a starchy shirt pocket and brought out a note. "Stuck under the motorcycle brake lever." Bohannon took it. It was in Spanish, and it said that Pancho was sorry to have killed the young man in the food truck. He asked forgiveness. Bohannon knew how he felt.

"The boy he shot," Bohannon said. "He's not dead?"

"He'll be fine." Gerard took back the note and laid photographs out on the table, color snapshots of a plumpish young woman and four young children, washed, combed, and in their Sunday best.

"These were in Pancho's wallet." He turned one of them over. "See that rubber stamp?" Bohannon saw it—the name of a camera shop in Havana. Gerard said, "He had a Mexican passport and a green card, but he'd bought them someplace, fakes. The CIA has his fingerprints. He's a Cuban, not a refugee, a Castro man, in this country illegally." Gerard gathered up the snapshots. "Maybe Williams knew that, and was blackmailing him or something."

"Can't you find Williams?" Stubbs said.

"He never lights for long." Gerard pushed the note and snapshots into his shirt pocket. "He's stayed at three different motels in the area in the past three days. Only once was he Williams. He was Johnson first, then Freeman. When he rented that compact, he was Barnes. No such address."

Rivera said, "What will happen to the poor bear?"

"The San Francisco zoo is sending a man and a truck," Gerard said. "Meantime, he's a prisoner in cell eighteen."

Gerard drank his coffee and left. Rivera went to muck out stalls. Stubbs to coach a pair of young girls in low jumps inside the white rail paddock. Bohannon cleared the table, set the soiled dishes in the sink, went along the hall to collect the girl's plate. It lay on the chest of drawers. She herself sat in a stiff rocker and reproached him with her eyes. "You weren't going to notify the sheriff."

"It wasn't about you," he said, "it was about my rifle. The man who came after you stole it. I went to get it back. There's a carnival in town. He worked for the carnival." Bohannon picked up her plate. "He had a trained bear act. Did you ever see it? The Tango Bear?"

She shook her head. She seemed honestly puzzled.

"He tried to kill somebody with my rifle." Bohannon gazed out the window down the canyon. "A man who calls himself Williams. Badly crippled up. Walks with aluminum crutches." Bohannon looked at the girl. "Him I think you do know."

She shook her head again, but too quickly this time, and fear showed in her eyes.

"He scares you senseless, he got me beaten up, and got a college boy shot at the carnival."

"I never wanted that," she said sharply.

"Then put a stop to it," Bohannon said. "Tell me what it's all about. Worse can happen. It already has. Tell me."

"I can't." It was a desperate cry, and tears ran down her scratched face. "You're lovely and kind and caring, and I want to tell you, because I know you'd understand. But I can't." She wiped at her tears with thin fingers. Her laugh was despairing. "That sounds stupid, doesn't it?"

"The Tango Bear man is dead," Bohannon said gravely. "When he couldn't get you out of here, when he couldn't kill the man on crutches, he killed himself. He had four small children and a wife back in Cuba. He's dead. Now, let me put it to you—whose fault is that?"

She reddened. "That's a terrible thing to say."

"It's a terrible thing to happen," he said.

"It isn't my fault." She jumped up. "Look—lend

me money. Drive me to Fresno, the airport. I'll go. You won't have to worry about me anymore."

"I'll worry about you anyplace but right here."

"They wouldn't find me," she said. "They'd give up."

"Pancho didn't kill himself because Mr. Crutches is somebody who gives up." Bohannon opened the door. "You stay here till I can stop him, okay?" He turned back. "A slim, distinguished-looking man with a neat gray beard. Does he mean anything to you?"

She turned away, shaking her head. "Please. You have to stop asking me questions. No—I don't know him."

"You're a liar," Bohannon said, and left the room, and shut the door behind him.

Sorenson knew him. Sorenson showed up in a bright red fire patrol car at noon. He and Bohannon had been young deputy sheriffs together. When he came into the kitchen, he found Bohannon at the table, working on accounts payable with an electronic calculator. A very old portable typewriter was at Bohannon's elbow, for writing checks and, later in the day, granted the luck, tapping out bills. At the other side of the table, Stubbs used a Blackwing pencil on a Strathmore drawing tablet. He would make a few lines, lift the pencil, look at Bohannon.

"Pale eyes," Bohannon muttered, scowling over the little white keys of the machine. "Blue or hazel. Pale, anyway."

Stubbs drew for a minute and held up the pad. "This him?"

Bohannon said, "What?" impatiently, then looked up and eyed the drawing critically. "More hair. He's got a good head of hair for a man his age—for a man of any age. That's about it, except for the hair."

Sorenson rattled the aluminum screen door. And Bohannon noticed him at last. Stubbs turned around on his chair. Sorenson had a long, horsey face and an aw-shucks smile. "It's hot out there. Thought you might spare me a beer. Been driving around trying to get people to cut back their brush. No rain in sight yet. Getting drier every day."

"Help yourself," Bohannon said, and bent over his bills again. Stubbs's pencil whispered on the rough paper. Sorenson opened the refrigerator, found a brown bottle, closed the refrigerator and, twisting the top off the bottle, ambled to the table, a gangly man. He peered over Stubbs's shoulder. "Hey, that's very good," he said, and rattled chair legs on the planks, and sat down. "What's it for?"

"Rivera's going to take it down to the carnival," Stubbs said, "and see if anybody there can identify him."

Sorenson's eyebrows went up. "You mean you drew that without even knowing who he is?"

"From Hack's description." Stubbs held the pad up to study it. "Never tried it before. Came out all right."

"It's a work of art." Sorenson tilted up the bottle and drank half its contents. He set the bottle down with a sigh. "Ah, that hits the spot." He took the pad from Stubbs and admired the drawing. "You going to give it to him?"

"If he wants it." Stubbs shrugged. "If we can find him."

Sorenson gave back the pad. "Try Solar Research Labs."

Bohannon stopped shuffling papers. "Up on the ridge?"

"He works there." Sorenson swallowed beer again, wiped his mouth with the back of his hand. "Dr. Farquar. I meet him on the road pretty often. Drives a big new Mercedes. Hard to miss. Always smiles and waves. Nice fellow."

"We'll see," Bohannon said.

It was the far ridge, the one that separated the cool of the coast from the heat of the inland valley. The buildings were plain white, big tilted saucers and dark, sundrinking slabs mounted on the roofs. Chainlink fence surrounded the place, topped by curls of razor wire. A severe signboard read SOLAR RESEARCH INSTITUTE, and in smaller letters gave information about whatever government agency in Washington, D.C., had charge of it. Uniformed soldiers stood outside the gates with guns, and inside the gates with guns. Signs fastened to the gates said ADMITTANCE RESTRICTED—U.S. GOVERNMENT INSTALLATION. Bohannon stopped the pickup at a white plywood kiosk by the gates. It was a day for meeting old friends. Ruhrig looked out at him, a retired deputy.

"Hack," he said. "You got permission to go inside?"

"I didn't know I needed it," Bohannon said.

Ruhrig took off his security guard cap, and wiped sweat off his bald dome with a puffy hand. He smiled sadly. "You gotta have clearance, Hack. This here is a top secret outfit. You gotta fill out forms. They gotta be cleared with the Defense Department." He peered with bleary blue eyes. "You ever kiss a girl? Ever pee outdoors? No way a man of your depraved character will ever get in here."

"I just want to see Dr. Farquar," Bohannon said. "Don't they allow visitors?"

"You want to visit," Ruhrig said, "guess they figure you can visit after work hours."

"Do you know Farquar?" Bohannon said. "When does he get off work? I'll wait out here."

"He didn't come in today. Yesterday, either."

Bohannon dug out his wallet, and from it took a business card. "Can you get this to his secretary or somebody? I want him to call me." He reached out the pickup window. "Let me have a pen." Ruhrig found a pen on an untidy shelf inside the kiosk, and handed it to Bohannon. Bohannon wrote *Urgent!* on the back of the card. He passed card and pen to Ruhrig. "If he shows up or telephones in to his office, maybe they'll put him in touch with me."

"I'll send it inside," Ruhrig said. He read what Bohannon had written. "What's it about?"

"I wish I knew," Bohannon said. "Maybe he'll tell me."

A shadow fell across Ludlow's apple orchards, taking the shine from the leaves and the young fruit. Bohannon frowned up through the dusty windshield. Sure enough. Wind was moving clouds in from the ocean. He gave a little smile. With luck, the dry spell was about to end. Sorenson could stop worrying about people cutting back their dry brush, and Bohannon could stop worrying about his horses. Taking the long loop of rising trail around the little valley, he watched the cloud shadows cross sloping grassland, where stocky whiteface cattle browsed.

The road began a steeper climb. He shifted gears. The mossy oaks and shadowy creek of the canyon bottom dropped away, the apple orchard, the grazing cattle, the coolness. He was in rock and dry brush country now, and the sun glared hot through the windshield. The windshield spider-webbed. A bullet plunked into the seatback beside him. He ducked. It was a no-good reflex. He didn't want to stop. If you were going to be a target, be a moving target. He crouched over the wheel, gripping it with the only good hand he had, and he throttled the old pickup hard, weaving from side to side of the narrow road.

This time he heard the slap of the gun. So the bullet had missed him. The next bullet spanged off the metal of the truck bed before he heard the gunshot. The road made a sharp angle. He braked for a second, then hit the throttle hard. Roadside dust swirled up. The right rear wheel almost went over. Then the road topped out. He could see well from here. He risked slowing for a minute to take a look. At first the world looked empty of anyone but him. Then sunlight winked off glass. He dimly heard the slam of a car door. He located it, among scrub oak on a rise—the beige compact. The noise of its four little cylinders starting reached him on the quiet air. The car lurched down toward the road.

Bohannon jumped out of the pickup, lifted the seat, dug a hammer from among rusty tools there, and knocked a hole in the crackled windshield glass so he could see to drive. He put hammer and seat back, scrambled into the cab, kicked off the floor what loose glass he could, and slammed the door. He let go the handbrake and drove on. He knew these canyons, every twist and tack. He would soon lose Williams.

To sneak home by crooked back trails would waste time, but he would arrive breathing. The girl had made breathing important to him again. She needed him. He had just begun to grasp why. And how much. The clouds blocked out the sun, now. Their whiteness began to smudge. The wind took on a cold, damp edge. He hoped a storm was the worst that was going to happen tonight. But he didn't believe it.

It was bad enough. By four-thirty rain fell heavily. It brought night early to Rodd canyon. Stubbs herded the last of the horses down from the pasture in near dark. A rubber poncho had kept the old man from getting wet, but nothing had done that for the horses. It was an hour before Stubbs and Rivera had dried them off and closed the doors on the last of the box stalls, and come into the kitchen where the girl sat and watched Bohannon cook. He had told her about Williams shooting out his windshield.

"If you get rid of me, he'll stop," she said. "Take me where I can get a plane."

"They won't be flying tonight," Bohannon said.

Thunder crashed, lightning flared, the wind rose and grew hoarse, shaking the ranch house. In the middle of supper the lights went out. After supper, Bohannon took the girl to her room with a kerosene lamp. He locked the window, drew the curtains, and left her with Rivera, the rifle, and chess pieces set out on a little table between them. Stubbs hurried back to the stables.

Bohannon washed the dishes by lamplight, set out files and forms on the table, and began to type statements, leaning close to the old portable to read what he typed. It was nearly eight by his watch when the screen door hinges creaked and knuckles rapped the wooden door. Bohannon went and pulled it open. Farquar stood there in a pale fly-front raincoat, rain-darkened on the shoulders. Rain dripped from the brim of his waterproof hat and from his neat gray beard.

"You wanted to see me?" he said.

"Come in," Bohannon said. Cold wet air blew in with the man. The doorway lit up with a lightning flash. Bohannon closed the door. Thunder split the sky overhead. Bohannon said, "Let me take your coat. Sit down."

Farquar shook his head, read his watch. "I'll stand, thank you. I'm running late. What is this about?"

"A man with crippled legs who calls himself

Williams." Bohannon got the Old Crow from a shadowy cupboard, and brought the bottle and two glasses to the table. "He tried to kill me today. I thought you could explain why."

Farquar looked around at the gently lamplit room. "What would make you think that?"

"You were talking to Williams last night at the carnival. By the burrito truck. When there was a shooting, you and Williams vanished. Together. Who is he, Dr. Farquar?"

"I'm afraid you've mistaken me for someone else."

"If that were so," Bohannon said, "you wouldn't be here. Sit down. Have a drink. It's a good night for it. Why did Williams come here the other morning to scout my place.? Why did he send someone to break in here that night? Why did that same messenger then try to kill Williams at the carnival, and having failed to do that"—Bohannon poured whiskey—"kill himself? I'm talking about Pancho, the bear trainer."

Farquar was silent. Bohannon looked at him. Farquar's paleness and startlement were plain even in the poor light. He took hold of a chair back, as if to steady himself. He said faintly, hoarsely, "Dear God. You've got her. Here." He looked over his shoulder, and he was afraid. He stepped around the table and the hand trembled that he laid on Bohannon's shoulder. "Where is she? Bring her to me at once."

"Not 'How is she?' " Bohannon handed him a glass. "She broke an arm and sprained an ankle jumping out of your car over yonder the other night. Wonder is she wasn't killed." Dumbly Farquar accepted the glass. Bohannon raised his. "Here's to fatherly concern. She is your daughter, right? She's got your eyes. Down to the fear in them."

"You're wasting time." Farquar set his glass down and headed for the inner door. "Jennifer? Where are you?" He opened the door and shouted along the hall. "It's Daddy. Please be reasonable, now. You must come with me."

"Where?" Bohannon stood behind him.

"To Europe. I've been appointed to a fine position there." He pulled airline tickets from a pocket and waved them helplessly. "She doesn't want to go."

"Emphatically," Bohannon said, and saw light fall into the hall from her room. She came out, stood for a moment staring, then hobbled slowly toward her father. "I won't," she said. "You know I won't."

Farquar said, "But Williams will kill you."

"Why would he do that?" Bohannon said.

"It could all have been so simple." Farquar sounded ready to weep. "Why wouldn't you just come quietly? Now it's turned to a matter of life and death."

"It was always that." She put her arms around him, kissed his cheek, pushed away from him. "You go. You'll be all right. You'll have what you wanted."

"But there's no reason why you—" he began. And stopped with a small cry. Williams came out the door from the girl's room. He had the Winchester clutched under his arm. "Young ladies Jennifer's age," he said, in a country-western twang, "don't always take to what's reasonable."

"That's no excuse to murder them," Farquar cried.

"He doesn't need excuses," Bohannon said. "It's his way of life. What's it about, Mr. Johnson-Freeman-Williams-Barnes? If you think she's given away your secret, you're mistaken. She hasn't said one word."

Short legs scuffing on the boards, big shoulders heaving, Williams came on with a grin and a chuckle. "You just didn't ask the right questions. There's folks who know how." He jerked the rifle barrel at them. "Get in the kitchen, please? Where we can all be comfortable?" The thunder cracked again, echoing down the canyon. Williams told Bohannon's back, "You serve up some weather, here."

"It's my father's secret," Jennifer said. "I won't betray my father. Even though I think he's wrong. But you can't understand that, can you? You can go your way in peace, Mr. Williams. So can he."

"I like to be very sure," Williams said. "Sit down." She sat. He stood. "Dr. Farquar, you are not going to be on flight 709 to Berlin if you don't start pretty soon. San Francisco's quite a drive in the rain."

"Let me take her," Farquar begged.

"Get a move on, doctor," Williams said softly.

"No. Not without Jennifer." Farquar dug frantically in his coat. "I won't leave her here to die." A little black revolver was in his hand. He caught the girl's wrist and brought her up off her chair. He backed toward the kitchen door, she hobbling beside him, eyes wide with fear in the lamplight. She looked terribly young. Williams fumbled with the rifle. Bohannon blew out the lamp.

The rifle blazed. Its explosion was deafening. Bohannon dropped to the floor. The kitchen door opened. A gust of wet wind blew across the floor. Lightning flashed, and by its glare Bohannon located Williams, who was struggling to cock the gun again. "Run like hell," Bohannon shouted, lunged low at Williams, and knocked his crutches from under him. The man fell. The rifle clattered. Bohannon groped for it, found it, tottered to his feet. Williams got a grip on Bohannon's ankle. The man was strong. Bohannon used the rifle the only way he could with one bad arm, the way Pancho had used it on him—as a club.

He wheeled a rented car into the yard at sundown two days later, switched off its engine, and sat looking at the place, the long, low-roofed white stables, the fences, the trees, the browsing horses in the meadows newly greened by the rain. He was grateful to be back. He got stiffly out of the car and breathed the fresh air deeply. The smell of law-enforcement buildings was about all he'd breathed for forty-eight hours. From San Luis to Sacramento, where the CIA had offices. He knocked heels along the porch and opened the kitchen screen door. Stubbs was at the stove.

"Not turkey hash again," Bohannon said.

"You hurt my feelings," Stubbs said. "It's beef stew."

Rivera rose from the table to fetch a plate and eating utensils for Bohannon. The boy looked pale. His head was bandaged. When he had risen to follow the girl out of the room after she'd heard her father's voice, Williams had hit him from behind. "I am ashamed," he said.

"Forget it." Bohannon sat down. "Bring me a glass with ice and the whiskey, all right? And I'll tell you all about it. I don't want any questions. I've done nothing but answer questions ever since I left." He sighed, lit a cigarette, and took the glass and bottle Rivera brought. "And I'll have to answer them all over again down the line when there's a trial." He poured himself a drink.

"Who's Williams?" Stubbs said. "A Roosky spy?"

"Don't do that," Bohannon said. "Just listen. Williams works for Williams. Near as I can gather, anyplace and everyplace in the world. He's a broker. He buys and sells."

"Secrets? Did Farquar pass him some kind of new weapon they been working on up at that solar research place?"

"There you go again," Bohannon said. "Yes, but not for cash. For an ideal. To save humanity. He figured if both sides had this new horror, there'd be a standoff. Williams arranged for that post in East Germany. Farquar had quietly settled his affairs here. He was just going to disappear."

Stubbs took large bowls out of a cupboard. "Only his daughter found out. That how it went?"

"And confronted him, tried to persuade him to turn Williams in. Farquar might be excused, then. He wouldn't listen. And now he said she had to leave with him. When she jumped and ran instead, he panicked and told Williams."

Stubbs ladled the bowls full of stew. "And

Williams decided she had to be killed to keep her quiet. Couldn't manage it himself, so he sent the bear man. Why him?"

"Williams has a list of vulnerable people. Pancho was handy. Williams threatened his family back in Cuba."

Stubbs limped to the table and set down steaming bowls. "How's the girl? How did she take it?"

Bohannon had happened on her this morning in a courthouse corridor. She looked forlorn. He said, "Don't feel bad. You did what you thought was right. You did your best."

"It wasn't good enough," she said bleakly.

"It almost never is." Bohannon said.

Snipe Hunt

Outside, on the long covered boardwalk that fronted the ranch house, a cat clawed the aluminum frame of the screen door. It was morning. The wooden door stood open. Good smells filled the kitchen—of coffee, of sputtering sausage and slabs of cornmeal mush turning golden in cast-iron skillets. But it wasn't the hope of food that brought the cat. Something glittery dangled from his jaws. He was a big, black and white tom cat with massive jowls and clear, indifferent, yellow eyes.

"Should have named that cat Magpie."

Stubbs said this, a stocky ex-rodeo rider gone white in the whiskers. He came hobbling to the big deal table with plates of food that he set in front of Hack Bohannon, owner of this place, a boarding stable up a rugged canyon on California's central coast, and Rivera, a slender, dark youngster, studying for the priesthood at a seminary on a nearby ridge, who helped Bohannon out part-time.

"Or Pack Rat," Stubbs added, and went back to the stately white enamel and nickelplate cookstove for his own breakfast and a platter of sourdough biscuits. "No—Magpie. Them's his colors, same as the birds." He plunked down the plates, scraped chair legs on smooth planks, and sat down. His blue eyes took in Bohannon's plate. "Right. Sunny side up on the eggs again. I told you, it's the only way I know how." He took a biscuit in arthritic fingers, broke it open, buttered it. "Never claimed to be a chef. Just a chuckwagon cook is all. You want it fancy, cook it yourself, Hack."

"I will," Bohannon said. He often did. He filled his mouth with sausage, egg, fried mush, washed these down with coffee, and rose to go open the screen door. The cat came inside and dropped the glittery thing with a small rattle at Bohannon's feet. It was a wristwatch. Free of it, the cat was able to make a few remarks, and he made them. Bohannon smiled, said, "Thank you. Very nice, right." He bent, gave the sleek black and white back a couple of strokes, and picked up the watch. On the face of the watch was printed *Cartier*. Expensive. The cat crossed the room, and jumped up easily onto the counter beside the stove, to stick its head out and sniff at the hot pans there. Bohannon went back to the table, sat down, laid the watch next to his plate. It was undamaged. The time was right—ten past six. Bristles of dry grass were caught in the reticulated metal band.

"A nice watch," Rivera said.

"How far does he go, collecting things?" Bohannon said.

Rivera's slight shoulders moved. "Not far, I don't think."

"He likes his comforts too much," Stubbs said. "He sticks around the stables mostly. Mostly sleeps."

"He thinks he is a horse," Rivera said with a smile.

Bohannon doubted it. Eating now, drinking coffee, he watched the cat jump down from the counter and come to the table. He stood looking up first at Stubbs, who ignored him, then at Rivera, who shook his head, then at Bohannon, who nodded. The cat sprang lightly into his lap. Bohannon broke off a bit of sausage and set it between the cat's teeth. The cat growled as if someone was threatening to take the food away from him, and jumped down on the floor to eat it, still growling, shaking his head as if he had a mouse in his jaws. "He knows he's a cat," Bohannon said, "and he wouldn't have it any other way. I've got a theory. It explains the mystery of Man. Cats invented Man to look after them."

"I will tell the monsignor," Rivera said. "He has been giving us the wrong information."

"-feed them, shelter them, keep them out of trouble," Bohannon said. He frowned and turned the watch over. Initials were engraved on its back. "T.K.," he said, and looked at Stubbs's ruddy face and Rivera's smooth, brown one. "Mean anything to you?"

"Had a Mrs. T.K. here the other day," Stubbs said. "Rented Seashell and Mousie for a morning's ride. Young fellow with her she says was her nephew, but, she didn't look at him like a nephew. Mrs. Thomas Kruger. She didn't give me the boy's name."

"The first time?" Bohannon asked.

"First time with him," Stubbs said. "But she's

been up before. New little red roadster. Mostly with women her own age, women friends. Middle forties. Rich women. Time on their hands. Lunch afterwards, I expect. Lots of margaritas."

"With the girls," Bohannon said. "Not with the nephew."

"No, she'd find something else to do with him," Stubbs said, "if memory serves me."

"I think"—Rivera pushed back his chair—"the conversation is slipping from its usual high spiritual plane, here. There is work to do." He rose, smiling a little. "Among our speechless friends, the horses, who are God's innocents, and will not trouble my mortal thoughts."

"Sorry about that," Bohannon said.

"Stay and offer a prayer for that nephew," Stubbs said. "Woman looked like a man-eater to me."

"I will see you later." Rivera went down the room to the screen door. When he pushed it open, the cat slipped out between his boots. He followed it, and the door rattled shut. Stubbs sighed, belched softly, used his napkin. "Fine day. Wasn't for the annual giant community rummage sale and flea market in Madrone, we'd be busy. Maybe I'll run down there myself, later. I could use a couple new shirts." He rose, started off, paused, glanced back at Bohannon, and changed course. From a cupboard, he took down a gray mottled cardboard file shaped like a shoebox, and limped to the table with it. "Her number will be in here."

Bohannon was pouring coffee. He nodded his thanks. But no one answered the telephone at the number Mrs. Thomas Kruger had given Stubbs.

Bohannon finished off his new mug of coffee and two more cigarettes, went to the wall phone and tried the number again. It rang in an empty house. Not even an answering machine. Bohannon went along a knotty-pine hallway to a plank bedroom where Rivera had earlier made up the poster bed under its patchwork quilt, as he made the beds every day. Bohannon pulled on socks and boots, checked the kitchen stove to see that Stubbs had turned off oven and burners—he sometimes forgot—then went out into the bright morning and his pickup.

The cat in fact went far afield. Bohannon clattered the old GM along a lot of dusty back trails and side canyons before he caught a glint of metal down among brush in a barranca sheltered by big old oaks. He braked, climbed out, slammed the door with a clang that echoed in the stillness, and slipping, sliding, scraping hands and the seat of his britches, followed the slurred swath a car had made chuting down here. It was a red European sports car of some kind that looked new. It rested on its top, wheels up. Bohannon crouched to see inside. Nobody. He straightened up and looked around. All he saw was dry brush and drier rock bleaching in a stream bed that wouldn't run with water until winter, when it would run hard and deep. Boots crunching rock, he circled the car, squinting against stabs of sunlight down through the dusty trees. A lizard scuttled away, claws whispering agitation in the stillness. It scampered over a shoe. Bohannon went for this, picked it up, saw a second shoe—and this one had a foot in it. A stout, gray-haired man in a pricy tweed jacket and wool trousers sprawled face down among boulders like something broken and thrown away. He had leaked blood, and flies buzzed around this. Bohannon crouched and touched a hand. It was cold. He climbed back to his pickup and used the two-way radio there.

Brown sheriff's department cars stood in a loose row along the back road half an hour later. Also a brown ambulance, a converted van with a row of lights along its top and an electroplated howler that glittered in the sun. Men in chalky lightweight jumpsuits toiled up the slope with the body of Thomas Kruger in a zippered bag on a gurney with its shiny tubular metal legs folded. Deputies in crisp suntans nosed around the red car, took photographs, used a steel tape for measurements. It took Bohannon back to where he had no wish to be anymore. He'd been a deputy for fourteen years and loved it, and then had come to hate it, and had quit. Because people kept coming to him for help, he held a private investigator's license now, but he wished they would stop coming, would forget about him, leave him alone. He was content with the horses, for the same reason as Rivera, he supposed. They were innocent. Human beings were rarely that—himself least of all.

"Lieutenant?" A young deputy with freckles called this from beside the car. The call went echoing down the canyon. Someplace far off, as if answering, a crow cawed, and another. The man beside Bohannon grunted and went skidding, teetering down to the freckled kid. The man was Gerard.

Bohannon had worked with him for a long time, and they had been friends—until Gerard was part of a whitewash that let an officer get away with shooting dead an unarmed Latino boy in Cayucos. Now they were civil when they met, but that was the extent of it. Bohannon followed Gerard. The young deputy said, "I don't think it was an accident, sir. It looks to me like the brakes were tampered with. A slow leak in the line. Back at the garage, we'll be able to tell for sure."

"Somebody wanted him to drive off the road?"

"I'd say so." Up on the road, the doors of the ambulance slammed. The kid lifted his head, squinting in the sun glare. "Yes, sir."

"It's a stupid plan for murder," Bohannon said. "Too much could go wrong. Why would someone try it?"

Gerard shrugged. "Money? He was well off. Senior vice president of Mountain Savings and Loan."

"What was he doing driving up here?" Bohannon asked.

"Looking at land?" Gerard wondered.

"It happened in the dark," the young deputy said. "His headlights were on. The doc said the body temp makes it someplace around midnight when he died."

"Not looking at land," Gerard said, and turned to Bohannon. "You know all these canyons. What's here, who's here?"

"Nothing and nobody," Bohannon said. "And he wasn't heading over the ridge for Atascadero or Paso Robles. Not on this road. Anyway, he was pointed back. Only it would take him a hell of a lot of chopping and changing to get there."

"Maybe he was lost." The young deputy wiped

sweat off his forehead with a hand. "But why come so far to get lost?"

Bohannon said, "Maybe somebody lied to him."

"A snipe hunt?" Gerard said. "I'll ask at the savings and loan. I'll ask his wife."

"She's not home," Bohannon said. "I tried the number twice this morning."

Gerard frowned. "You knew who he was before you even found him? You want to explain?"

"My cat brought this in at breakfast time." Bohannon dug the watch out of a frayed Levi's pocket and laid it in Gerard's hand. "His initials are on the back. Stubbs took a stab at guessing what they stood for. His wife rides my horses sometimes."

"Why would she lose his watch for him?" Gerard said.

"Exactly what I asked myself," Bohannon said.

"You found the answer," Gerard said. He ventured a smile, and in a country-western twang repeated something they used to say to one another when they'd worked together young. "You done good, son."

Bohannon kept his face stiff, and felt sad and angry. There was no use in Gerard's trying, even less use in Bohannon's encouraging him. It could only be fake now. Up on the road a truck engine rumbled, gears clashed. Bohannon winced and peered upward. The wrecker had arrived to winch the pretty little red car out of the barranca. He said, "I don't think that's his car. I think it's hers." He started up the steep slope, rubble rattling down behind him with each step. "Let me know what happens."

But it wasn't Gerard who let him know what happened. It was a very young woman in baggy white sheeting pants and jacket yards too big for her, a Union 76 blue and orange globe printed on her T-shirt, and panic in her eyes. Bohannon was waiting under the overhang of the white and green stable building while a young father leaned against the wall, writing him a check for riding lessons given. It was late afternoon. The kids seemed relieved the lesson was over. They were about nine or ten. The blond one had grabbed the dark one's hat and was running and dodging with it, and jeering. Out in the yard, with its white rail fences, flower beds, shaggy old eucalyptus trees throwing long shadows, the girl had hopped out of a new compact and was talking shrilly to Rivera, pushing at her crazily cropped pale hair, and waving her arms. The young father tore the check out of its folder, handed it to Bohannon with a wan smile, pushed the folder away, and went to collect his boys. Bohannon tucked the check into a shirt pocket. Rivera pointed, and the girl came running to Bohannon, jogging shoes, no socks.

"You have to help me," she panted. "You have to."

Bohannon took down a bucket from a nail beside a box stall door. "Why me?" He walked away with the bucket.

She ran alongside him. "Mr. Fitzmaurice said you would."

"Archie?" Bohannon bent to a tap and turned the

valve. Water splashed into the bucket. "Are you his client?"

She shook her head. "Melanie Kruger—that bitch."

Bohannon glanced at her. He turned off the tap and set the bucket down. "Mrs. Thomas Kruger?"

The young woman nodded. She licked her lips and eyed the water in the bucket. "They arrested her. At the rummage sale. For killing him—her husband. Last night."

Bohannon frowned. That was fast, wasn't it? He said, "But you call her a bitch, so it isn't her you want help for—her and Archie."

"No, it's Dennis," she wailed. "Dennis Toomy."

Bohannon couldn't stop a small smile. "Would that be her nephew? The one she came here with the other morning?"

"Her nephew!" She scoffed. "Is that what she said? Oh, wow! What a hypocrite!"

"There was a husband." Bohannon took a dipper off a hook, plunged it into the bucket, brought it up filled, offered it to her. "Thirsty?" She took the long handle and drank, water dribbling off her chin, darkening the 76 globe between her pert little breasts. She handed back the dipper and wiped her chin with a hand. Bohannon hung the dipper up again above the tap. "If he isn't her nephew, what is he?"

"A graduate student at Davis—an arboriculturist. Trees, all right? And when she drove in for gas the other day, Mrs. Kruger told me about her oaks dying, and I said maybe Dennis could help her, okay? So she called the university, and he went, didn't he? And what does she do—invite him in. For lunch. Oh sure, for lunch." Hurt and disgust were in her voice.

Bohannon's mouth twitched. "Those things happen. It's his age. And hers. Don't take it too hard."

"I'm liberated," she said. "but it wasn't just once. He kept going back. She gave him presents. He's a poor boy. A Rolex watch, gold chains, a camera? Why wouldn't he?"

"Not for love?" Bohannon said.

She stared, outraged. "Have you seen her? She's old."

"He left you for her," Bohannon said.

"I'm not jealous," she said stoutly. "Is that what you think? Well, you're wrong." An old bay gelding called Bearcat put his head out over the closed lower half of his stall door and nibbled at her puffy windbreaker. She jumped. "Hey!" Bearcat, who had a sense of humor, lifted his head, curled his upper lip over long yellow teeth, and nickered. Bohannon laughed and led her two steps out of the horse's reach. Then he held the water bucket up and, shaggy black mane falling into his eyes, Bearcat drank—noisily, splashily. The young woman said, "I just hated seeing her using him. I knew it would lead to trouble. I went and begged her to leave him alone. She sneered at me. Now look what's happened."

Bohannon set the bucket down. Bearcat grabbed his hat by its brim. Bohannon grabbed it back, grinning, and gave the big soft muzzle a push. "Get in there and behave yourself," he said. And to the young woman, "What has happened?"

"They've arrested him too. They say she paid him to murder her husband." She waved her small hands. "But he didn't do it, Mr. Bohannon. He couldn't."

Bohannon's brows rose mildly. "Paraplegic?"

"Stop that. Of course not. But he's not that kind of boy. I've known him all my life. He's gentle. He can't hurt anything living. He wouldn't. Kill another human being? Never." She shook her head fiercely. "Never."

"The sheriff doesn't make arrests for murder without a reason. What's the reason?"

She stopped looking at him. She turned away to watch or pretend to watch Rivera helping an old couple down off horses. Both were rail-thin. They wore black Mexican outfits with silver braid, silver belts, silver bands around black gaucho hats. The saddles on their palominos were heavy with silver. Once the couple must have cut a dash, but they were frail and stiff in the joints now, and Rivera had a time of it to keep them from breaking bones dismounting. The young woman said glumly, "The sheriff has letters they wrote. And her check made out to Dennis. That he cashed."

"What kind of letters?" Bohannon said.

"What kind do you think?" she asked bitterly.

"I see." Bohannon sighed. "I don't see what I can do. It sounds open and shut to me. I'm sorry."

She turned to him sharply. "Don't say that. He didn't do it." Tears filled her eyes. "You have to help him."

"What's Mrs. Kruger doing?" Bohannon said. "Keeping Arch Fitzmaurice all to herself?"

"You better believe it," the young woman said.

"He'll have a public defender then," Bohannon said. He touched the girl's shoulder. "Don't worry about it. If he didn't do it, it will come out at the trial."

She shrugged his hand away. "No, it won't. She'll blame it all on him. She'll say it was his idea." Her laugh was sour. "Haven't you ever heard about one law for the rich, one law for the poor? She'll get away, he'll go to death row."

"When you're older," Bohannon said, "you'll learn that things almost never turn out as badly as we fear."

"Don't patronize me," she said. "I tell you— Dennis didn't do it. I know he didn't. There—is that good enough for you?"

Bohannon looked away, over her tufty blond head, past the yard where the shadows had stretched, purple on the yellow hardpan. A breeze had risen, as it did about this time every day, bringing coolness and a smell of the sea. It rustled the high trees. Over the canyon rim, colors other than blue began to change the sky. Soon it would look like the inside of an abalone shell. Then it would streak with reds and, almost before you could blink, it would be black and strewn with stars.

He asked, "Are you being very careful with your words?" He looked into her eyes. "What makes you so sure?"

She dropped her gaze and her voice. "I can't tell you." Then quickly she looked up again, and gripped his arms. "But I am sure. I swear it. Now, will you help him—please?" She poked into a pocket of the blowsy white jacket and brought out a wallet. "I'll pay you. I have a job." She held out two twenties. "And I can always sell my car, if I have to."

"Let's see if I'm any use first," Bohannon said. "What's your name? Where can I find you?"

"Billie Shears," she said, and gave a Madrone address.

Rivera looked wounded in his feelings and shook his head. "Next time, you must take one of us with you," he said. He dipped a fragment of fried tortilla into a big bowl of guacamole, and stuffed his mouth with the green stuff. "You are an artist." Chewing, he nodded at Stubbs's drawings on the kitchen walls—horses mostly. When the weather was warm and dry and his joints weren't too stiff from arthritis and old breaks, Stubbs liked to draw and he did it well. "But you have no taste in clothes." Rivera washed down the food with orange soda. "That is a terrible shirt."

Stubbs worked at breaking long elastic strings of white Mexican cheese. Bohannon had fixed beef enchiladas with his own secret sauce and the cheese melted on top. Holding a forkful of enchilada high, Stubbs sawed at the strings of cheese with a knife. He glanced at Rivera. "For any man that can drink that stuff with perfectly good food to talk about taste," he said, "don't add up to much." He gave up, laid the knife down, stuffed his mouth, and wrangled the cheese strands in as best he could with the fork. He looked down at the shirt. "It's got all its buttons. It covers me up decent. What's wrong with it?"

"It makes you look like a sofa," Bohannon said.

Outside in the red sunset light a car door slammed, steps sounded on the porch planks, a figure appeared at the screen door. Knuckles rattled the frame. "Hack?"

"Come in." Bohannon stood up and started for the stove. "You want supper? Enchiladas."

"They give me heartburn," Gerard said. "Thanks. My wife will be expecting me." While the screen door rattled shut behind him, he read his watch. "Jesus, it's late. But I wanted to fill you in." He moved a chair out at the table and sat on the chair. "If you've got a beer around . . . "

Bohannon took down a glass and brought a brown bottle from the refrigerator. He set these in front of Gerard and resumed his place and his eating.

"I seen you arrest that Kruger woman," Stubbs said. "Right in the middle of the rummage sale she was running. Surprised hell out of folks. Even me."

"Oh, then it's not news," Gerard said. He tilted the glass and let beer run out of the bottle slowly into it. He regarded Bohannon. "What more do you want to know?"

"How come it happened so fast?" Bohannon said. "Did you settle on her first, or did you find those letters first?"

Gerard tasted his beer, smacked his lips, wagged his head in appreciation, and read the label on the beer. "Anchor. It's still the best, isn't it?" He reached across, picked up the orange soda bottle, shuddered, set it down again, and asked Rivera, "How can you drink that stuff?"

"It is an old Aztec tradition," Rivera said.

Gerard said to Bohannon, "The mail gets to my house about eight-thirty. A brown envelope was in the box, and my wife noticed that it didn't have any stamps on it. Also it seemed a little damp, and the rest of the delivery didn't. As if it had been in the box all night. She phoned me about it, and I sent a car around for it. And it had these letters in it—from this Davis student, Dennis Toomy. And I phoned the Davis police, and they went around to ask questions of Toomy, and they found Melanie Kruger's letters to him. And they fit together. They made a picture."

"Love letters?" Stubbs said. "That the nephew?"

"If you'd stayed here instead of going shopping for awful shirts, you'd know all about it," Bohannon said.

"Love letters of a sort," Gerard said. "Sex letters is more like it. But with a nasty turn to them. All about how wonderful the world would be for this twenty-three-year old kid and this forty-five-year old woman if only her husband was dead. She couldn't leave him, because he'd cut her off without a dime. And she didn't have any money of her own. He wouldn't politely divorce her. It would disgrace him. So wouldn't it be nice if he met with some kind of fatal accident."

"No specifics?" Bohannon said.

"Better than that. A check for five hundred bucks. The D.A. is delighted. To any jury the meaning has to be plain, in the light of what happened to Kruger. He doesn't figure to have any trouble with it."

"Billie Shears is having trouble with it," Bohannon said.

"That pest," Gerard said. "Was she here, too?"

"She's very much in love with young Toomy."

"Yeah, well," Gerard grunted, "love is blind." He

gulped his beer and filled the glass again. "How did she happen to hunt you up? What does she expect you to do?"

"Get the boy off," Bohannon said. "She must have pestered Archie Fitzmaurice, and he sent her to me to get rid of her." Bohannon finished his enchiladas and laid down his fork. "Who left those letters in your box in the middle of the night?"

"Kruger himself," Gerard said. "We asked neighborhood dog-walkers. Heavyset, middle-aged, white-haired. Who else could it be? Before he drove off to die. Ironic, isn't it?"

"You said he didn't want a scandal," Stubbs said.

"If the county prosecuted her for conspiracy to commit murder," Gerard said, "what could he do about it? It wouldn't reflect on him—and it would punish hell out of her."

"If you want proof there is a God"—Rivera rose and went into gathering shadows to fetch the coffee pot from the stove—"just look at how miserably people act without Him."

"I want to talk to Toomy," Bohannon said. "Who's his public defender?"

"May," Gerard said. "Fat Freddie."

Madrone was a cluster of spindly, jigsaw-work houses in foothills above the coast highway. The houses had been fixed up inside, and outside painted candy colors. A good many of them now housed antique stores, gift shops, small restaurants. The names were quaint and quaintly painted on swinging signboards. The sea wind creaked them a little tonight. He saw the gilt lettering spark through the drooping branches of fine old roadside pepper trees. The main street had showed a lot of dull brick storefronts not long ago. Now these had been covered by cedar and redwood planking, so the street looked like a set for a western.

Bohannon made a face, and rattled the old pick-up onto the lighted tarmac beside the pale brick sheriff's station. He parked in a slot reserved for official vehicles, and pushed the heavy glass doors into the place grimly. He hated coming here, hated the smell of the place, the familiar sounds echoing down familiar hallways from familiar offices. The officer at the desk, with a padded phone at one ear and a slim tubular microphone at mouth level, was a dark young woman, slightly bucktoothed. She raised thick, dark brows above lustrous eyes, and sketched a smile for him.

"Hack Bohannon," he told her. "May's expecting me."

She widened the smile and pointed down a hall. "Interrogation room." She glanced at a wall clock. "He has Dennis Toomy with him." She tilted her head. "He must have known you'd be on time. Are you always?"

"You can test me," Bohannon said. "Tomorrow night. At six-thirty. The Briary Bush. Dinner? They serve great steelhead steaks there—fresh caught from the creek."

She laughed, a sound pleasant as bells. "And they charge twenty dollars for it. Are you rich, Mr. Bohannon? Can you afford to throw your money away on nameless deputy sheriffs?"

"Your name is T. Hodges," he said. "It's on your badge."

She touched the badge with slim fingers. "I'd forgotten that. Who are you? What do you do?"

"Keep stables up Rodd canyon. For town people who haven't anyplace to keep a horse. I also rent horses to people who can't afford them but like to ride."

She watched his left hand scratch his ear. "That's a wedding band." Her glossy brown eyes mocked him.

He said stiffly, "My wife's in a mental hospital." Linda had been held hostage on a filthy drug smuggler's boat, half-drowned, beaten, and repeatedly raped. Afterward she had crept inside herself—it looked like forever. "I'm not asking you to sleep with me, deputy. Only to have dinner with me."

A telephone with a broad, flat display of lucite buttons on her desk began to buzz and wink. She said, "Perhaps some other time," gave him a gentle, regretful smile, pushed one of the buttons, picked up the receiver and spoke into it.

Bleakly, Bohannon walked to the interrogation room. Fred May was twenty pounds heavier than he used to be, which brought him to about three hundred pounds. He also had less hair. But the tic that tended to make jurors wonder if he was serious when he pleaded with them and kept winking—that seemed gone. He wasn't dressed for a courtroom tonight. He wore a blue T-shirt stencilled SAVE THE SEA OTTER, and his belly bulged over cut-offs bought when he was thinner. His arms and legs were furry. He sat at a scratched yellow oak table on a bentwood chair his bulk made appear fragile.

Across from him sat a big-boned blond boy, long hair pulled back in a 1960s ponytail. He wore yellow jail coveralls, unzipped to the navel, showing a deep chest, gold hair glinting on it in the sour overhead light. The sleeves of the coverall were short, and the boy's arms were thickly muscled, gold hair glinting on them too. With his big, strong hands, high cheekbones, blue eyes under a heavy brow ridge, he looked as Paul Bunyan must have, just out of the egg. What he failed to look was bright.

"What's this all about?" he said to Bohannon.

"Billie Shears wants me to help you." Bohannon pulled out another bentwood chair and sat on it. He looked at Fred May. "How can I do that?"

"If I was going to kill him by fixing the brakes on a car," Toomy said, "I'd fix them on his, not hers."

"Not if you knew she'd be using his car last night," Bohannon said, "to haul things over to the park for the big yard sale. Lieutenant Gerard says she was doing that all day and the better part of the night. His is a big car. Hers is too small for the purpose."

"I didn't know about the sale," Toomy said.

Bohannon looked at May. May shook his head. The white, bare top of his scalp shone greasily in the light. "He says he was in Davis, but I can't scare up a witness."

"I was in my room," Toomy said. "Studying. I'm doing my masters, now. I'm going for a doctorate." He looked ready to cry. "I should have gone to the library. Then everybody would have seen me. I go almost every night."

"Is there a phone in your room?" Bohannon said.

"Nobody phoned me," Toomy said. "I wish they had. It's a wall phone, down the hall. The landlady answers it, and calls anybody that's wanted."

"You didn't call out?" Bohannon said.

"I told you—I was studying," Toomy said.

"But you keep a stock of quarters," Bohannon said, "so you can call when you need to. Madrone, for example. The Kruger house?"

Toomy's mouth twisted. "I keep a stock of stamps," he said with grim humor. "We wrote letters."

"So I hear," Bohannon said. "But somebody telephoned Mr. Kruger last night. That's how it looks. And lured him up into those canyons above Madrone, where he drove off the road and died because the brakes on his wife's car had been monkeyed with. All the fluid dripped out."

"I don't know anything about cars," Toomy said.

May unwrapped a stick of chewing gum and folded it into his mouth. "That checks out. We had the Davis police ask his friends on campus. Dennis is famous for his ignorance of mechanical matters." He gave the boy a brief, unhappy smile.

"All the letters say," Toomy told Bohannon, "is how great it would be for Melanie and me if Tom had an accident and died. They don't say anything about rigging an accident."

"You use the library all the time," Bohannon said. "What would stop you from looking up in an auto repair manual where the brake lines are? They're easily accessible. Anyone could poke a hole in one with an ice pick."

"I don't have an ice pick," Toomy said. "What kind of helper are you supposed to be, anyway?"

"You wanted him dead so you could live off his widow—the money, insurance, property she'd inherit. That's a motive, Dennis. It would help if someone else had one. Didn't Melanie ever mention anybody else who'd want Tom Kruger dead?"

Toomy gave his head a shake. "All she said was Mountain Savings and Loan was his whole life. He'd forgotten about her, years ago—never took her anyplace, hardly spoke to her. His focus was down to making money." Toomy sulked. "Greed. It's ruining the planet."

"And that's why you killed him?" Bohannon said.

"I didn't kill him," Toomy shouted.

"What was the check for, then?"

Toomy flushed. "It was a gift. She said I needed clothes. That's how she is. Beautiful and fine and giving."

"Uh-huh. You should have stuck to Billie Shears." Bohannon looked at May. "Has bail been set?"

The fat man nodded. "Fifty thousand each."

Bohannon asked Toomy, "Have you got five thousand bucks for a bail bondsman?" Toomy only stared. "Because if you haven't, you'll stay locked up till your trial."

"That's not true. Melanie's not like that. You don't know her." But Toomy's bravery was all noise. He turned to May and his voice was small. "She wouldn't leave me here."

May chewed his gum. "She walked out an hour ago."

"You're no use to her anymore, Dennis." Bohannon rose. "But don't take it too hard." He went to the door. "Billie still loves you." He pulled open the door. A uniformed officer waited outside. Bohannon turned back. "Billie says she knows you didn't do it. How does she know that?"

Toomy said dully to the table top, "Figure of speech."

"I hope not," Bohannon said.

Bohannon remembered this place as a meadow. He recalled a particular afternoon, though it may have been several afternoons overlaid in his memory and probably was, when twenty or more deer had come out of that stand of oaks over there, hesitant, watchful, big ears moving, and stood statue still in knee-deep spring grass and wildflowers, watching his car pass. Sunset time it had been really. Now it was bright morning, and in the meadow stood three large houses. The building-over was happening fast. Before he died, Rodd canyon, too, would have filled up with people, houses, kids, dogs, cars. He'd move on when that happened—though God knew where he'd move to. He swung in at a curving driveway between patchy new lawns and flowerbeds, and halted behind a white BMW parked at the front door of the house.

The woman surprised him by being small and slim. *She's old,* Billie Shears said in Bohannon's memory. But she did not look old. She was as fair as Billie, or fairer, her hair in a fashionable short bob. She wore jeans and a plaid shirt and soft leather boots, and carried a glass of orange juice. To his question, "Do deer come down out of those woods anymore?" she answered without surprise, "Yes, sometimes, still. It's the raccoons that give trouble, though." Her smile made age lines around a generous mouth. "What bandits they are." She looked him up and down. He wore jeans too, and a plaid shirt, and boots, but all of a tougher sort and not new, like hers—far from new, in fact. His hat was mapped by stains of sweat and weather. She frowned a little, which didn't make her look younger, either. "You own the riding stables, don't you? What brings you here?"

"I'm also a private investigator." He took out a folder and showed her his license. "I'm inquiring into your husband's death." He looked into her eyes. They were greenish gray. "I'm sorry for your loss."

"Thank you." She said it mechanically, dismissively, and turned from the doorway. "Come in. I'm glad you came. Something's wrong here. I was about to phone the sheriff."

The house was New England saltbox, gray and white outside. Inside it was comfortably formal, the furniture traditional. There was a lot of wallpaper and white paint. The staircase had varnished treads. He closed the door behind him. "Wrong how?" he asked, and she led him up the stairs. She opened a white door to a rear room the designer probably meant to be slept in but that was outfitted instead with a desk and file cabinets, a computer in glossy beige plastic, a multi-line telephone, shelves with books about banking and finance. He saw what she meant by wrong. Drawers hung open, papers strewed the hardwood floor, the oval braided rugs. She had showed him inside past her. She hung back, standing outside in the hall.

"He didn't like me to come in here," she said.

Bohannon looked around at the mess. He turned

back to her. "Those letters Dennis Toomy wrote you. Did you see them when they questioned you at the sheriff's station?"

"Oh, yes," she said glumly, "yes, indeed."

"And they had all of them? There were no others?"

She shook her head. "I still don't know how Tom found them. He wasn't the suspicious type. He trusted me. They were hidden in a small department store gift box in my closet." Her smile was amazed. "You didn't think I'd hide them here."

"I didn't," Bohannon said, "but someone else might." He pushed at computer printouts with his boot, frowning, listening to them rustle. "Have you had break-ins before?"

"Never," she said. "Of course, we only moved out here a few weeks ago. But it's not common in this area, is it?"

"You think it happened last night?" Bohannon crouched, picked up an armload of the folded sheets, and squinted at them. "What made you look in here this morning?"

"I came home tottering with exhaustion after Archie arranged my bail," she said. "I showered to get the smell of the jail off me, took a sleeping pill, and slept very hard. It was early, but I didn't care. I wanted oblivion. But sometime in the night I woke. Had I heard someone in the house? I didn't know, and I fell asleep again right away. But when I got up this morning, I remembered the noise. And I looked through the house. Not thoroughly, really. I half thought I'd dreamed it. But that's how I happened to look in here."

"So it could have happened the night he died, when you were both away," Bohannon said. "Or during the day."

She shook her head. "No. I have a daily woman. Inez."

"Right." Bohannon let the printouts whisper onto the desk, and studied the room. "He brought work home. So where is his attaché case?"

Startled, she came into the room, orange juice glass still in her hand. "That's a very good question." She walked around, peering into corners, into a closet stacked with storage files and office supplies. She shut the closet door and regarded Bohannon. "Private investigator? Working for whom?"

"Dennis Toomy," he said, "at the request of Billie Shears."

"That brat," she said coldly.

"What was in the attaché case?" Bohannon asked.

"Good God, how would I know? Me—a mere woman?"

"What did it look like?" Bohannon said. "Color, make?"

"Mark Cross. Tan cowhide. With his initials in gold. I gave it to him for his fiftieth birthday. It was something he took with him everywhere. I thought"— she sounded for a startling moment as if she might cry, and tears brightened her eyes—"he might be reminded of me now and then."

"Do you think Dennis Toomy arranged for that accident?"

She shrugged fragile shoulders inside the plaid

shirt, and turned away. "What a fool I was. A college boy. Dear God." She walked out the office door, halted, turned back. "The things loneliness can make a person do. How I wish I could change it, go back to that morning, not feel what I felt, just let him look at the oaks and tell me, and then send him on his way. I'd give everything to change that."

"I know what you mean," Bohannon said, and he did. "But do you think he went ahead and fixed those brakes? Do you think he telephoned your husband here that night, while you were out hauling tarnished toasters and lopsided lamps down to Seaside Park for the sale, and told him something that would get him up into those mountains, those canyons, those crooked dark little trails at midnight?"

She opened her eyes wide. "Wait. Maybe the attaché case was in the car. He could have taken it with him. Maybe that was what whoever called asked him to bring."

"Did Dennis know anything about your husband's work?"

"All Dennis knows is trees," she said.

"The attaché case wasn't in the car," Bohannon said.

"Perhaps after the crash, the killer took it."

"Afraid not," Bohannon said. "I was the first person to come upon the car. There were no human tracks down there. I don't think he took the attaché case." Bohannon came out of the office room and closed the door behind him. He told her, "You think Dennis did it. That's why you left him in jail."

"He's emotional," she said. "A child. I shouldn't

have wept on his shoulder. He hated Tom for what he'd done to me. But I never meant for him to—" She closed her mouth.

Bohannon grunted and started down the stairs. "It's a beautiful house," he said. "A beautiful setting. A way of life most people only dream about. You forgot all that?"

"Exactly," she said. "I was a fool."

"And Dennis Toomy has to pay?" Bohannon stood on the polished oak floor of the entry hall and glanced into the handsome lifeless rooms on either side, morning sunlight slanting into them. "It wasn't Dennis who rifled those files upstairs."

"I suppose not." She shrugged, passed Bohannon, pulled open the front door. She gave Bohannon a wan smile as he put on his hat and stepped outside. "I don't want to think about it. I'm a selfish, spoiled woman, used to having everything—almost everything—as I want it. I want to forget Dennis Toomy. All about him. As quickly as I can. If I can." She used the woebegone smile to mock what she knew herself to be—though she didn't really care. She laid a hand for a moment on Bohannon's arm. "He'll be all right. You don't think he did it. You'll find out who did."

"You broke it," Bohannon said, "and I pick up the pieces?"

"Something like that," she agreed.

He thought of Rivera. "You don't believe in hell?"

"Oh, yes," she said. "It's right here on earth."

Merritt Fletcher rocked in a highbacked padded rawhide chair behind a glossy desk. Executive director of Mountain Savings and Loan, he was a hefty man in his mid-fifties, white-haired, rosy-cheeked. His blue eyes had a way of twinkling, and laughter seemed always ready to shape his mouth. He didn't have Thomas Kruger's taste in clothes, however. His linen jacket was a loud plaid in rust red and three shades of green. Fletcher said:

"She could have rifled those files herself. Why not? I've known Melanie Kruger for years. Close friends with a man, close friends with his wife, right? But I never liked her. Had no reason for that, so I tried to overcome the feeling." He sighed, and waggled white eyebrows. "But now, it looks as if my instincts were right. She blamed Tom, said his career left no time for her. It wasn't that way. She was cold, cold as she looks. I'd have divorced her. I've done that twice. Not Tom." Sorrowfully, Fletcher shook his head. "For him, she was the only woman in the world. Poor bastard. What else was there for him but his work?"

Bohannon said, "She could have done it herself, yes. To furnish Archie Fitzmaurice with an argument in her defense—that somebody else wanted Tom Kruger dead."

"It wouldn't have worked for long," Fletcher said.

"That's why I don't think she did it," Bohannon said.

"Rifled Tom's files, you mean," Fletcher said. "She killed him all right. Nobody else had a reason."

"He had a lot of work at home, there," Bohannon said. "Stuff he'd brought from here."

Fletcher sighed, lifted big, expensively kept hands, and dropped them to the desktop again. "I tried to interest him in golf, tennis, sailing—I have a boat: he was always welcome. 'All work and no play,' I told him, 'will kill you, Tom. You have to learn to relax.' But he didn't listen. You're right. He took mountains of work home. Had a computer set up there, interfaced with our system here."

"Right," Bohannon said. "And what would somebody break in and steal. Why would they?"

Fletcher lifted beefy shoulders. "Can't imagine. I mean, if this was a high-tech manufacturing business, a research laboratory, yes. But we're a simple savings institution. Nothing of value but our integrity."

Bohannon rose from the leather chair that faced the desk and went to gaze out a window. Across the highway below, the tall, lean pines of the hills that hid the ocean swayed in a forenoon wind. The sun was bright, the sky blue. "You know," he said carelessly, "drugs come in on this stretch of coast. On supposed fishing boats? Illegal aliens with cash to pay the fare? Money changes hands. That money has to go someplace, if only to wait to be sent south for laundering."

"Now, listen here." An angry flush replaced Fletcher's rosiness. "If you're implying—"

"Relax," Bohannon said. "I didn't mean you knew where the money came from. But suppose some of it is here? Suppose Tom Kruger discovered some customer, maybe more than one, has been making bigger deposits and withdrawals than he could explain?"

"Ah, yes, I see. Sorry." Fletcher's anger seemed

to subside, though wariness lurked in his eyes. "Putting it like that, maybe you're right. But there's this college boy. Those letters between him and Melanie."

"I don't think the break-in took place at the Kruger house till after Tom Kruger was found dead, and they were arrested. It worries me, Mr. Fletcher. It worries me that Tom Kruger's attaché case is missing."

"It worries me," Fletcher said with sudden heaviness, "that Tom is gone. I'm going to miss him terribly. Not just here, where I relied on him, his sharpness, his honesty. We were close as brothers. Family. We had keys to each other's houses, could talk anytime, about anything, and did."

"Who broke into his house? What for?" Bohannon said.

Kruger's phone pulsed softly on the desk. He lifted it, listened, said "Right away," hung up the receiver and rose. "I don't have any idea," he answered Bohannon, "but you can be sure I'll look into it." He touched Bohannon's card that lay on the desk, a horse head printed on it. "And if I find anything the least suspicious, I'll get in touch with you." He let his smile loose now, a little ruefully. "Meantime, I'll ask you to excuse me. The State auditors are here on their semi-annual visit." He shook Bohannon's hand, pulled open his office door, and with a hand between Bohannon's shoulder blades, showed him out, and turned his attention to bespectacled men in poplin suits, who came in carrying attaché cases.

The sea had done nothing for it, nor had the nets, nor the long fall with thousands of glistening fish into a wallowing boat. It was wet, scuffed, scarred, but the initials T.K. still gleamed gold in the hard light of Gerard's office. The case gaped empty on his desk. Empty except for one thing. A Smith and Wesson .45 revolver. Bohannon stared.

"Who belongs to that?" he said.

"Kruger's wife–widow–the ice princess says he never owned a gun," Gerard said. "Not of any kind. He gave money to the anti-handgun movement."

"Circumstances alter cases," Bohannon said. "It looks new. If he bought it recently, maybe it means he felt threatened. Maybe by the people who broke into his house and stole the briefcase—and whatever was in it."

"It is new," Gerard said. The corners of his mouth twitched in suppressed amusement. "I just put it back in the case to show you how the fishermen found it. It's been through the lab. The cylinder was full. There are no fingerprints on it. If they were drug dealers or coyotes, do you think those types would throw away a brand new name-brand gun? That had nothing incriminating about it, not a bullet fired?"

"I don't think so." Bohannon picked the gun up. It was cold and damp because the suede lining of the attaché case still held water. He turned the heavy thing over in his hands, puzzled, and laid it back in the case. "Why would anyone?"

"A call will come in on the registration soon," Gerard said. "But what was in that case before the gun got there?"

Bohannon wasn't listening. He frowned out the

window, where patrol cars sat in the parking lot, and big eucalyptus trees rose out of ground-lighting into darkness. "Emotion," he said, "revulsion. When I was about ten, I stole a handful of cigarettes and sneaked out to a storage building full of rusty old tools and cobwebs to smoke them. I got through maybe three and, Goddamn, was I sick!" He laughed at the memory. "I looked at the ones I had left, and took and threw those suckers as far as I could into a corn patch. I never wanted to see another cigarette."

Gerard grinned. "Happened to you too, did it?" His face sobered. "Yeah, I see what you mean. Somebody bought it to kill with, and lost his nerve."

"Somebody with a boat," Bohannon said.

"Not a smuggler. They don't give a damn what they do."

Bohannon said grimly, "Tell me about it."

"Sorry," Gerard said. "So—who does that leave?"

"One man," Bohannon said. "Merritt Fletcher."

Gerard's brows went up and he blinked. "Director of Mountain Savings and Loan? Are you serious?"

Bohannon said, "You could ask him. He owns a boat. He wears jackets that belong only one place— where horses run and horses' asses bet. Auditors were due at his bank today. Last night somebody stole papers from the office in Kruger's house. In that attaché case. Why hadn't Kruger found out Fletcher was embezzling to cover his losses at the track?"

"Jesus." Gerard said it softly and looked pale. "You think it was Kruger who did the phoning—

said I've got this proof you're creaming accounts, and we better talk about it, and meet me someplace in the mountains at midnight?" Gerard reached for a telephone, said into it, "Terry, get me the harbormaster's office," and set the receiver down again. "If he went out last night to jettison that attaché case, maybe he was seen." Gerard closed the attaché case, snapped the catches, sat staring at it. "But he wouldn't dump the papers at sea."

"His house is that big white Gothic fright down on the point, alone there in the pines. It has a lot of chimneys. He probably used a fireplace."

"Probably." The phone rang. Gerard picked it up, and spoke to the harbormaster's office. And smiled. Yes, Fletcher took his boat out—around one A.M., and came back in an hour. Gerard hung up, pushed back his swivel chair on squeaky wheels, stood and picked up the attaché case. "You are one smart son-of-a-gun." He went to lift down his jacket from a hook by the office door. "Fletcher is going to love seeing this again."

"Did they see him carry it on board?"

"No. But I just remembered something." Gerard set the case down, and shrugged into his jacket. "He's a thick-set, fiftyish man with white hair, right?" He carried the case into the hall and Bohannon followed. Down the hall the clack of typewriters echoed, the moan of a siren from outside. Gerard stopped at the reception desk and told T. Hodges where he was going. She gave him a nod and Bohannon a long look he couldn't translate. Gerard led Bohannon outdoors, where a wind had risen, the smell of rain on it. He said, "Same type as Kruger."

"Meaning," Bohannon said, "it could have been Fletcher who left those letters in your mailbox."

"Stubbs was right," Gerard said, "it didn't make sense for Kruger to do it. He wouldn't have wanted a scandal."

"And Fletcher, on his way to kill Kruger, left the letters to cover his ass, to throw suspicion on the wife and her lover." Bohannon followed Gerard to the parking lot, bending into the wind. "Just one thing—how did he get hold of those letters?"

"I'll ask him." Gerard stopped beside a patrol car. "She went riding at your place with Toomy. I don't call that keeping the affair a secret, do you?" Gerard tossed the attaché case into the patrol car, got in, slammed the door. "She runs with a gaggle of idle rich women, close friends. Maybe she bragged about Toomy. Maybe she even showed off those letters." The worn engine clattered into life. "Women get carried away."

"They aren't the only ones," Bohannon said.

"What?" Gerard began to back the car.

"You're forgetting." Bohannon walked beside the car, wincing, holding the brim of his hat to keep the wind from snatching it. "Kruger wasn't killed with a gun."

"You're forgetting." Gerard halted the car. "Fletcher's gun wasn't fired. He lost his nerve, and fixed the brakes instead. That way, he wouldn't have to watch his friend die."

"You don't even know the gun is his," Bohannon said. "You're going too fast. Back off. He's a power in these parts. I don't want you tangling with him on a half-assed theory of mine. You could lose your job."

"Thanks." Gerard blinked at him soberly. "I appreciate that, Hack. But–" He backed the car fast, turned it sharply, tires squealing on the blacktop. The car rocked to a stop, the gears clanked. Gerard said, "I don't think it's half-assed. And I have to see what's in that fireplace." The car shot forward, jounced out of the parking lot, and roared away up the night street, where the tops of trees were tossing in the wind.

Rain had come on that wind, all right, but the storm had blown on past by midnight, and this morning the sky was a new-washed blue. Patrol cars crowded the sheriff's station parking lot that was still patched with rain damp and clumps of litter from the trees. But there was an empty slot, and Bohannon left his old pickup truck in it. The stationhouse smelled of coffee in paper cups. Officers stood in groups, drinking coffee, munching doughnuts, talking. Some of the older ones knew Bohannon and gave him nods as he went past. Gerard looked at him red-eyed, told him to come in and shut the door, told him to sit down. He halfheartedly lifted his Styrofoam cup and raised his eyebrows over it in a question.

"No, thanks," Bohannon said. "What was in the fireplace?"

"Very fine ash. I don't think the lab can make anything of it, but Fletcher thinks they can." Gerard smiled. "I don't know where he got that idea, but it was enough to make him talk."

"So he is a compulsive gambler," Bohannon said.

"You know that. His jacket told you. And you

know how that goes, don't you, for a man who handles other people's money every day. You know he heard about those letters from a woman friend, you know he had a key to the Kruger house so he could hunt till he found them, and then he could search Kruger's workroom and remove the proof that he, Fletcher, was ripping off Mountain Savings and Loan. And you know he removed the proof in that attaché case and burned the papers in his fireplace, and dumped the case at sea." Gerard snorted. "Half-assed theory? You were right on target."

Bohannon shrugged and lit a cigarette. "But?" he said.

Gerard held up a hand. "Wait. Let me finish reciting everything you know. You know he bought the gun. That didn't seem to me to equate too well—how could he have done that so fast? The answer has two parts. A week or more ago, Kruger had told him he'd run across irregularities that made him think someone inside the institution was draining off interest on accounts. At that point, of course, Kruger didn't dream it was Fletcher, but Fletcher knew, and it panicked him. That's when he bought the gun, on the pretext that it was to arm a security guard. But when he got it in his hands, he knew he couldn't use it. But you know that. The second part is that it was Fletcher who phoned Kruger that night. Just as you thought in the first place. He told Kruger he'd confirmed his suspicions, and asked Kruger to meet him you know where. But only to get Kruger out of the house, so he could sneak in and get Kruger's proof to destroy it."

"A snipe hunt." Bohannon smiled. "As you said."

"That's exactly what it was."

"Not exactly," Bohannon said. "Not if Fletcher tampered with the brakes on that little red car."

"Yeah, well," Gerard said gloomily, "that's where you missed the target and hit the cow."

"He couldn't have fixed the brakes," Bohannon guessed, "because he was out of town at the time? Left early, didn't get back until very late? How am I doing?"

"You're being too modest." Gerard drank from the white cup, made a disgusted face, said "Cold." He looked at Bohannon. "Tell me where he was. You know where he was."

Bohannon had to laugh. "Not Santa Anita."

"Give the gentleman a cigar," Gerard said. "And not alone. He picked up friends—one in Ventura, two in Santa Barbara. We've had them checked out. It's true." Gerard looked sourly into his cup and made to rise. "So, we're back at square one."

"I told you it was a half-assed theory." Bohannon stood.

"He's still an embezzler," Gerard said. "Around three hundred thousand, he estimates. You did a good thing, Hack. It helped a lot of people."

"It didn't help Dennis Toomy," Bohannon said.

The rain had washed the shaggy, drooping heads of the old pepper trees that sheltered the brick and glass filling station by the highway out of town. Above the trees on a tall steel pole the revolving orange ball with its blue and white 76 gleamed glossy as new. A bony man in crisp blue workclothes unlocked the office door of the filling station as

Bohannon swung the pickup in off the highway where there was little traffic yet, it was so early. The man had faded red hair and a worried look. He puttered at a steel desk for a minute, then came out and undid the padlock on a wide garage door that he swung upward. It looked almost too heavy for him. He went inside, puttered at a workbench there for a moment. Bohannon stopped the pickup and climbed down out of it. The man turned, called, "Help you?" and came at a quick walk.

Bohannon said, "Mrs. Thomas Kruger a customer of yours?"

The man tilted his head on a scrawny neck and looked doubtful about answering. Maybe he thought confidentiality existed between garage mechanics and their clients. Bohannon showed him his license. The man thought about it for a minute and said, "Both of them." He nodded. "Too bad, what happened." His naturally worried look deepened. "You think you know folks. You never know. I sure wouldn't have pegged those two for that kind of trouble. Plenty of money. Not a worry in the world." The mention of money reminded him, and he headed back to the office. Bohannon followed. "And damn if he doesn't drive off a road and get killed, and they're saying she did it—her and some college boy."

"That's what they're saying," Bohannon agreed.

The man crouched, slid back a panel under a counter, opened a safe there, and took from it packets of paper money and bags of coins. He closed the safe, rolled the panel shut, and carried the money past Bohannon and out to the slant-top steel boxes on posts beside the gas pumps.

"But maybe it wasn't that way," Bohannon said.

The man unlocked the first of the steel boxes and began laying bills into it, then rattling coins into it. "Did Mrs. Kruger leave her car here, day before yesterday—for a lube job, oil change, wheel alignment, something like that?"

"She didn't." The man closed down the lid of the first box, locked it, angled off to the second. He had a rickety walk. "He did. Says he was using her car because she needed his big one to haul stuff down to the park for the rummage sale." He clattered open the padlock on the second change box and glanced at Bohannon as he opened it. "Yeah, an oil change. That's what it was." He began laying in the rest of his bills and coins. "Said he'd pick it up at four-thirty—which is what he done." The man paused and looked again at Bohannon, startled this time. "Was that the car he crashed in?"

Bohannon nodded. "Little red sports car. Do you have a college girl working here, name of Billie Shears?"

"That's right." The man finished with the money, shut down the lid, locked it. "Part-time, is all. But she's a good little worker. Don't mind getting her hands dirty."

"Did she get them dirty on Mrs. Kruger's car that day?"

"Here she comes now." The man pointed. A new little hatchback curved down the offramp from the highway, windshield flashing in the sun. "You can ask her yourself."

"I'd rather you told me," Bohannon said.

The man tilted his head again, guarded. "What for? She do something wrong?" Bohannon said nothing. The man looked worriedly at the car Billie wheeled to a stop under a pepper tree, dry berries crackling beneath the tires. "Well, yes, she was the one. She wasn't here when Mr. Kruger left the car, and she was gone by the time he picked it up, but she was the one that worked on it. It'll be written on the repair bill."

"Good," Bohannon said. "Thanks for your help."

Billie Shears, in a clean blue jumpsuit with the 76 logo stitched to the pocket, flung herself out of the compact and came running. Her hair was still spiky. "Mr. Bohannon," she panted, "have you found out anything to help Dennis?"

"Morning, Billie," the filling station owner said.

"Oh." She gave him a quick, distracted smile. "Morning, Mr. Zimmerman." She peered up at Bohannon, anxious, begging. "It's me you're here to see, isn't it?"

"That's right," Bohannon said. "And the answer is yes. Just as you said—Dennis wasn't the one who fixed those brakes."

"Oh, that's wonderful," she cried, and hugged him.

"It was you," he said, and hugged her back.

Allowing for the heat, Stubbs had very early this morning made potato-leek soup, and now it was chilled through. They ate it with thick chunks of new-baked bread and a crisp white wine from a vineyard the other side of the mountains. They were alone at the noon kitchen table. Rivera was up at the seminary.

"The green-eyed monster," Stubbs said, "never dies."

Bohannon said, "And she isn't sorry. She'd do it again. She's a good hater for one so young." He gnawed a crusty chunk from his slab of bread, swallowed some wine, followed it with a spoonful of the icy soup. "Cool customer, that Billie—until Dennis was arrested. Then she lost her head."

"So, now he's free—does that make her happy?"

"Not with me, it doesn't." Bohannon glanced ruefully at his left hand. His old doctor friend, Belle Hesseltine, had cauterized, stitched, and bandaged it. But Billie had bitten to the bone. The hand ached and throbbed. "She hates my guts."

Footsteps sounded on the long porch, a slender shadow fell on the screen door, there was a light rapping. He told the shadow to come in, and a slight woman entered, the cat with her. In the backlight, it took him a moment to make the woman out. T. Hodges, in a crimp-brimmed straw hat, gingham shirt, trim jeans. Crouching to pet the cat, she smiled faintly.

"I thought it might be nice to ride a horse today."

Bohannon stood. "Have some lunch first." He pulled out a chair. "Then maybe we can go riding together."

Witch's Broom

"Did you ever win anything, Hack?" George Stubbs, stocky, ruddy-faced, white-stubbled, spoke from behind a newspaper at the table in the big pine-plank kitchen. "Here's a fella won fifty thousand dollars from the supermarket down in Morro Bay. Can you beat that?"

"I can't beat that." The windows stood open, letting in cool air that smelled of sage and eucalyptus. Beyond the windows and the long roofed walkway that fronted the house, the sky was blue over the tawny, brush- and rock-strewn slopes of the canyon. "I never won anything, no."

Breakfast was done with. Bohannon drank strong coffee, smoked a cigarette, and tended to the morning mail, frowning at bills, pleased by checks. A lean man of forty, he owned this place—boarding stables. He loved horses. It was a good life. Except that people wouldn't forget he'd been a deputy sheriff. They kept coming to him in trouble. He'd never worked out how to turn them down, so he held a private investigator's license. But he didn't much like those times. He rose now, picked up plates, carried them across wide planks to the sink. Out the window there, he saw horses browsing the meadows up behind the white and green stable buildings. Foals bucked on knobby-kneed legs, tossed their heads, chased their mammies. "Who was this lucky fellow? Anyone we know?"

"Name of Powell, Timothy." Stubbs claimed his eyesight was failing. After a long life as a rodeo rider, when he'd broken a lot of bones, he walked crippled up. Wet weather gave him rheumatics. But he didn't wear glasses, and he found Powell's address in the paper now without trouble. "Same mail route as us. I think I know him. Yup, his picture's here. He's rode our horses. That's right. Mother drops him off and picks him up. Way she watches him, he's her jewel."

"How did this contest work?" Bohannon laid a rubber stopper over the drain, cranked the hot water tap, squirted detergent into the rush of water. Suds foamed up. Steam clouded the window. "Does it say?"

"You had to shop every day in May, and keep your sales slips," Stubbs said. "They had a drawing, and the customer that got a total closest to the number they drew won the big prize. There was littler prizes—automobile, cruise of the Caribbean, video recorder, all kind of stuff."

Bohannon mopped plates with a plastic handled brush with plastic bristles, and set the plates in a rubber-coated wire dishrack beside the sink. "You didn't save our slips?"

"Hell, I never even knew about it," Stubbs said. "You do the shopping. Up to you to tell me. Must of had signs up in the market about it. Didn't you read 'em?"

"What they said to me," Bohannon said, "was 'Shop someplace else, Hack. If these people can shell out money like that, they're overcharging you.' "

"Maybe young Powell thought that, too," Stubbs said. "And now look at him. He collects tomorrow. Going to be a ceremony at the market, a band, balloons. He'll be on TV."

"Don't be jealous," Bohannon said. "You've been on TV. You've had your turn."

"That was just for living and remembering," Stubbs said. "Hell, I'd rather have fifty thousand dollars."

The inner door opened and Rivera came in, a slight young man, quiet, shy, who was studying for the priesthood, and paying his way by working part-time for Bohannon. Rivera had just made the beds, dusted, cleaned the bathroom. "Hack," he said, "can you come with me up to the ridge this morning? It won't take long. And I promised Monsignor McNulty."

"You ever win anything, Rivera?" Stubbs asked him.

"I never gamble, George," Rivera said. "My father was a gambler. Cards. It never helped him. It never helped any of us—except to keep us poor."

"Here's a young fellow, Powell, up the road someplace, won himself fifty thousand dollars from the supermarket in Morro Bay. What do you think of that?"

"I hope he gives some of it to the church," Rivera said. He went to Bohannon, filled a saucepan, sluiced hot water over the sudsy dishes in the rack. "Hack, will you come?"

"What's the matter?" Bohannon dried his hands. "Somebody drink the sacramental wine?" From a cupboard he took a tin tackle box, carried it to the table, opened it, laid the bills and checks inside. "The way to approach this would have been to ask me first—then promise the monsignor."

Rivera watched him put the box back. "I thought you were only anti-clerical on Sundays."

Bohannon laughed, and lifted a worn Levi jacket off the back of his chair at the table. "I'll come—it's okay." He shrugged into the jacket, picked up cigarettes and matches from the table, took his hat from a brass hook by the door, opened the door. "Come on. Let's go see what it's all about."

Monsignor McNulty said, "We'd never have noticed, if it hadn't been for the witch's broom." A tall, rawboned old man, in a clerical collar, the bones of his face stood out, the skin over them taut, red-veined. Wind ruffled his thick white hair. "We have to get it out of the oaks once a year, and spray them afterwards, or it will kill them."

He pointed to a metal ladder that leaned in one of the big trees that sheltered the graveyard. Well up the ladder, a pudgy, balding, bespectacled youth in T-shirt and jeans, red-faced, sweaty, plucked small sprouts of stiff, pale green growth from among the shiny oak leaves. He dropped the witch's broom into a yellow plastic bucket hung to an upright of the ladder. Sometimes. More often, he dropped the witch's broom to the ground. The monsignor peered at Bohannon with bright blue eyes from deep, hollow sockets under white brows.

"What do you make of it?" he asked.

Bohannon shrugged. "Same as you. Same as Rivera." The three of them stood beside a newly-dug grave, six feet long, six feet deep, with straight sides. The earth from the grave had been carefully covered with a blue plastic sheet, the corners of the sheet anchored by chunks of dry old adobe taken from the crumbling walls of the abandoned graveyard. "It looks like a professional job." Bohannon let his gaze rove the neglected place that was rank with brush, headstones fallen, the big oaks casting ragged noontime shadows. "But I don't know why, anymore than you do."

"The earth is soft here and easy to dig," Rivera said.

"And it's a place no one ever comes." Ireland echoed in the monsignor's speech. "These are old graves, you know, and the graves of men without descendants. Eighteenth century. Not a successful mission, it lasted a scant twenty-five years and fell to ruin. It was a century too late for restoration when the diocese chose this site for the seminary."

"The burial ground walls had fallen," Rivera said. "The rains had washed the rotted wooden coffins from the earth. The bones of the friars were scattered like chicken bones—as if these good men had never served God with their hands and hearts, as if they had never prayed. It was a crime."

"And now there's going to be another crime, it looks like." Bohannon pushed the weathered Stetson back on his shaggy dark hair. "It's new," he said to the monsignor. "You've questioned your people? No one saw anything?" Bohannon nodded toward the stark, yellow-brown buildings below, masked by a high, ragged hedge of eucalyptus trees. "No flashlights moving around up here in the dark?"

"Nothing like that," McNulty said.

"No bad blood between your young men?"

"Hack!" Rivera's brown eyes were soft as a deer's. They showed pain. "These are my friends. They will be priests. They have given their lives to God."

"Cain talked to God every day," Bohannon said, "face to face. He still turned out to be a murderer."

The oak trembled, the ladder rattled, a shower of witch's broom fell. Bohannon took a step, steadied the ladder, peered up against the hard blue sky into the shadows of the treetop. "You all right?" he asked the pudgy boy.

"Uh, fine, yes, all right," the boy stammered, and went back to harvesting the parasites with almost frantic zeal. The stiff little growths pelted Bohannon's hat. He stepped away from ladder and tree. The monsignor told him:

"We have cases of small envies, hurt feelings, rivalries." His look returned to the empty grave. "The usual human frailties." He worked up a slight smile for Bohannon. "We have no saints here. But I doubt we have a murderer."

"Forgive him," Rivera said, "he lives in another world."

"A world where we do have murderers." Bohannon bent and peeled a price tag off the blue plastic cover. "You'd better post a watch up here from now on."

The monsignor's white brows rose. "Day and night?"

"Whoever dug this will come back," Bohannon told him. "It hasn't served its purpose yet, has it?"

"It's a desecration of holy ground." The old man turned and began to walk away downhill. The underfoot was cloddy, rocky, loose, and he teetered on his long, frail legs. Rivera hurried to take his arm and steady him. The monsignor's voice drifted back on the hot air. "I'll have it filled in this very hour, and that will be the end of it."

Bohannon trudged after the old man and the young. "If you do that, whoever dug it will know it's been discovered. He'll dig another one someplace else we may never find."

"And if I don't"—the monsignor halted at the top of concrete steps in a thick retaining wall at the foot of the cemetery, built to keep more earth from sliding, more graves from opening and scattering their skeletons—"he will go ahead with his killing." He gripped Rivera's arm with bony fingers, and started down the steps, dry leaves crackling under his shoes. "And with his unhallowed burial rites."

"Make it a waiting game." Bohannon followed them down. "Keep the work going on the oaks, day and night. He'll hold off on his killing then, till the job's finished and the place is deserted again. It will give me time to find out who he is."

The monsignor shook his head. "It would be risking lives that are in my keeping. I couldn't do that."

"It is work for the sheriff," Rivera said.

The monsignor said, "They have already refused me. They came and looked. They think it's a schoolboy prank."

"Maybe somebody died a natural death," Rivera said. "In a family who could not afford a burial plot, a funeral. And still wanted them in a real cemetery, not out in some empty field, not thrown in the ocean."

"It would be the same," the monsignor said,

"without the sacrament. It would also break a good many laws of man."

"It sure as hell would," Bohannon said. "You know righteous people wouldn't do that, Rivera. Especially not poor ones. They find a way. They don't expect life to be easy."

"And criminals do." Rivera helped the old man onto the path at the foot of the steps. "I have often heard you say that. If it is true, why hasn't the murder already happened?"

"Because the grave's still empty," Bohannon said.

"I would like to help you," the monsignor said, "but—"

"I understand," Bohannon said. "I'll do it myself."

Madrone sat on hills along whose ridges horses browsed. It was a sleepy little town of spindly old frame houses with jigsaw porches that for a good many decades of this century had been let fall almost to ruin. Now they were all fixed up and painted candy-box colors and occupied by newcomers who had turned them into antique shops, fish restaurants, art galleries, real estate offices. Some of the houses were even lived in—those distant from the main street. Dogs slept on the main street. The buildings, once dreary brick, had been faced in cedar planks to give them a wild west look.

Bohannon parked his dusty pickup truck on the bias in front of the paint and hardware store where there was a roofed plank sidewalk. When he dropped down out of the pickup and slammed the door, he almost looked for Gary Cooper standing in the middle of the street with six-guns on both hips, but he didn't. He climbed hollow wooden steps, crossed the planks, and pushed into the store, where it was the '80s again, the 1980s, lots of shiny plastic packaging, very bright fluorescents, vinyl floors, Formica countertops. He moved up and down aisles until he found what he wanted. Then he hunted up a clerk in a green jacket, a thin, sun-burned, fiftyish man, testing a fishing rod back of a counter, dreaming.

"You sell a lot of these?" Bohannon asked.

The man put the quivering rod back in a rack with others like it and unlike it. "How many do you want?"

"I don't want any," Bohannon said. "I wonder who bought one from you in the last two days." He laid the folded blue plastic drop cloth on the counter, took out his wallet, showed his license. The man peered at it through thick glasses, then into Bohannon's face.

"Everybody sells these," the man said.

Bohannon showed him the price tag from the one up in the graveyard. "The one I need to know about came from here."

"They're useful for a lot of things," the man said. He poked a finger at the package. "You see here? They've got these brass eye holes, right? You can tie them over a car to keep off the rain, the sea spray. Lot of people do that. Wrap yard trash in them—they're cheap and strong. Cover up stuff you want to store outdoors. Put them under a sleeping bag. Lash them over a boat. We sell them for drop cloths for painting. But there's no end to what you can use them for."

"I can see that," Bohannon said. "You sell one lately?"

The man gave a little laugh. "Oh, probably half a dozen."

"Ah." Bohannon pushed his wallet away. "All to one man?"

"No, no. Different folks. I don't remember. It's not like you were asking who bought a certain color paint. I'd remember that. I'd remember them. But these things." He flapped knuckly hands in the air. "They're all alike." He peered at Bohannon again. "You're the fellow owns the stable up Rodd canyon, aren't you? Used to be a sheriff?"

"Yes," Bohannon said, "but I don't know you."

"I'm Dudley's brother Lloyd," the man said, "up from Lompoc. Dudley's in the hospital. Little minor surgery. Hernia. Occupational disease with veteran hardware men. You think you can lift it, and you're not as strong as you once were. Dudley's older than me. Ten years older. I'm just filling in for him for a few days."

"Give him my good wishes," Bohannon said.

"I'll do that. This something to do with horses," Lloyd wondered, "or something to do with lawbreaking?"

"Lawbreaking," Bohannon said, "maybe. Maybe whoever bought that dropcloth bought a mattock, a spade, a long-handled shovel. Does that jog your memory?"

Lloyd frowned, pursed his lips, shook his head. "Only one I remember is Professor Thornbury from the college. Dropcloth, couple gallons interior paint, sheepskin roller is all."

"Do you know his address?" Bohannon said.

"Have to ask at the college," Lloyd said, and

turned back to the rack of fishing rods. When Bohannon was almost out the door, the hardware man called after him, "But it's not a him—it's a her. Roberta Thornbury."

The college sat in a bowl of hills. Cattle had browsed the hills and the shallow valley only a few years ago. But Bohannon didn't resent the college. He had only squeaked out of high school himself, but he was a man who liked to read and respected knowledge and those who had it and those who had the gumption to try to get it. And the college looked right for the place—not in the stage-set way of the main street in Madrone, but the designer had hinted at adobe style without going overboard, so the buildings looked both old and new in a combination that didn't draw attention to itself. The color was right, the same brown as the summer hills.

He found a slot in the faculty parking lot marked on its bumper stone in black stencilled letters THORNBURY, and parked the pickup there. In an office, one of whose walls was an arched window looking on the hills, a woman who with her back to the early afternoon sunlight looked young but on closer inspection was past fifty, her girl's face webbed with a fine tracery of lines, told him Roberta Thornbury was on compassionate leave— as if the professor was a soldier in wartime. The corridors that had led him to this office teemed with youngsters so loud and lively they might be thought of as enemy troops if you were an embattled teacher with a lecture room full of them—they seemed an unlikely lot to try to contain.

"Somebody in the family sick?" Bohannon asked.

"Her father," the woman said. "Dying. I don't envy her. He was never an easy man when he was well." She found a pen, wrote the Thornbury address on a memo pad, tore the slip off the pad, passed it to Bohannon. "Like a lot of scholars, indifferent to the world around him, indifferent to the living, absorbed in the past, infinitely caring—for the dead."

"What was his field?" Bohannon folded the slip of paper.

"Local history, the Indians, the Franciscan missions," she said. "Fra Junipero Serra. He wants to live to see Serra made a saint. I hope for his daughter's sake that happens soon." She sighed, smiled. "Well, she's big and strong and unflappable. She's used to him. I suppose they'll be all right."

Bohannon put on his hat, lifted the folded slip to her, gave her a smile and a thank-you, and walked out the office door into hallways as empty and silent as they'd been crowded and noisy only minutes ago.

The Mexican graveyard outside Madrone on a flat section of high ground with a view of the sea and the sea wind always blowing across it and the cry of gulls—the Mexican graveyard always looked festive. It had a low picket fence painted white as many times a year as it needed it. So did a good many individual graves, whose headstones often had niches for photographs of the one buried there. But the festive look was due mostly to the flowers. Not every grave, but most of the graves were decorated with bouquets. The flowers were always fresh and bright because they were not real, they were plastic. Driving up a narrow lane that cut between sections of graves, Bohannon tried to remember when such flowers had first come on the market, and couldn't remember how the Mexican graveyard had looked before that time.

He spotted three men hunkered down beside a mound of earth. A wheelbarrow stood by, shovels lay by, a mattock. None was new. But one of the blue plastic tarps lay folded in the barrow. One of the men was bony, gray-haired, stooped. Bohannon knew him by sight. He did all the grave-digging in this area. The two with him were hardly more than boys. They had their shirts off. Both were brown-skinned, one was plump, the other muscular. Bohannon left the pickup on a gravel drive and walked over to them across tough, springy, well-trimmed grass. They watched him. All three smoked, all held beer cans in rumpled brown paper sacks. Bohannon heard the surf wash the shore below. Far off, sea lions barked.

"Buenos dias," he said. "My name is Hack Bohannon."

The old man squinted up at him against the strong light. "I know who you are," he said in Spanish. He flicked his cigarette away across the lawn, and stood up, slowly, as if all his years of digging had left him permanently in pain. "How can we be of assistance to you, Sheriff?"

"I'm not a sheriff anymore," Bohannon said, "but they've got a little mystery up at Santa Lucia seminary, and I'm looking into it for the monsignor. Maybe you can help me."

"The sheriff has no time for this mystery?" the

old man said. The youngsters got to their feet, put out their cigarettes under their work shoes, picked up tools. The plump one went at loosening the earth halfway down in the grave with the mattock, swinging it well and truly. Then he climbed out of the grave, and the muscular one jumped down and shoveled out the loosened earth. He passed the shovel up, took the spade, and chopped at the sides of the grave, straightening them. The old man watched for a minute, then turned back to Bohannon. "It seems unimportant to the sheriff?"

"It may seem important to him later," Bohannon said.

"What can I tell you, *señor*?"

"Did anyone hire you or your helpers here to dig a grave lately—other than here, I mean?"

The old man frowned. "Up at the seminary?"

"In the old, deserted cemetery where the monks were buried in the old days." Bohannon nodded. "That's right."

"I did not know there was such a place," the old man said.

Bohannon nodded at the sweating boys. "You want to ask them? Maybe they got an offer on their own."

The old man shook his head. "Jose is my son, Raymondo is my sister's son. They live at my house. They would have told me. Why not? It is a strange and interesting thing."

"Sometimes young men feel a need to be independent," Bohannon said. "At a certain age, they no longer wish to share all they know with their families." He stepped to the grave. "Did anyone pay you lately to dig a grave behind the seminary?"

They stared at him. "Seminary, *señor*?"

Bohannon pointed inland to the mountains, the ridge where the windows of the seminary winked sunlight through treetops, and small roofs glowed red. "Those buildings, where young men study to be priests? Long ago, there was a mission there, and the graveyard where the friars were buried is still there. No one hired you to dig a grave in that place? At night?"

They glanced at one another, looked guardedly at the old man, turned their black eyes back to Bohannon, said in unison, "No, señor," and went back to digging.

The old man said, "Someone dug such a grave?"

"Then left it empty," Bohannon said. "The monsignor can't understand that. Can you?"

"It is hard work to dig a grave," the old man said, "and it takes skill. Who would waste all that time, all that effort? Who would dig a grave and leave it empty?"

"Nobody," Bohannon said. "That's what's got me worried." He took a card from his wallet, a card with a horse-head decoration, and put it into the old man's earth-crusted fingers. "Telephone me if you hear anything, will you? *Gracias.*"

Across the coast highway from Madrone, pine-covered hills cut off sight of the ocean. Close together as they grew, building had started among them long ago. First city people down from San Francisco, up from Los Angeles, had put up summer cabins. Then retired folk had built year-round houses along the twisty roads, in the quiet woods, half hidden away. The pines were tall, long-needled, a breed to themselves, none quite like them anywhere else on earth. Shallow rooted, quick to grow, they were as quick to fall. Power outages were common in Settlers Cove. No one minded much. The cool, shadowy privacy, the nearness to the shore, made up for it. But those days were past. The trees were being brought down now by axes and chain saws. Sewers were in. The sounds of saws and hammers rang through the woods all day. Empty lots sold every day, and at very high prices. Old-timers were worrying whether to stop on and die here, or to sell out and try once more to find elsewhere the wilderness they were losing where they'd thought to stay forever.

Bohannon found Flurry Road and the mailbox marked THORNBURY and a brown-shingled place with decks back among pines and a thick, rust-red undergrowth of poison oak. He rolled the pickup up a ramp of patchy gray blacktop, halted it facing a double garage under the house—its doors up, an old, if shiny, Volvo parked on one side, among tools, stacked cartons, hanging bicycles, bedsprings, and on the other side a sporty new Jeep Cherokee with fake wood paneling. That one he knew—it belonged to Dr. Belle Hesseltine. He got down out of his truck, slammed the door in the silence, making a blue jay squawk among the high pines. He walked into the garage. A plank workbench ran along one side—dusty, not used for a long while. Tools hung in rows against the wall above the bench. They'd begun to corrode. Among them were small picks and light hammers—at a guess, archaeologist's tools. In a cobwebby corner leaned rakes, shovels, brooms, ax, mattock, spade. The cobwebs were torn. He knelt. The earth on spade, mattock, and shovel wasn't damp, but it wasn't so dry it flaked off either.

"Hack? What are you doing?"

He looked up, stood up. A stringy old woman in crisp blue jeans, gingham shirt, windbreaker jacket, stood in tennis shoes in the garage doorway, frowning at him. "It would take half an hour to explain," he said, and brushed the dirt from his hands. "You spare a half hour to listen, Belle?"

She snorted, walked to the Cherokee, tossed her kit inside. "You know better than that. I came up here to Settlers Cove to retire. Never had a busier ten years in my life. And it gets worse." She climbed into the new car, slammed the door, and looked strictly at him out the window. "You're not going to stir up trouble for Roberta Thornbury, are you?"

He looked innocent. "Do I ever stir up trouble?"

"Every time you decide to play Good Samaritan," she said. "What's it about? She's got an old man in there dying, who's as mean as any man that ever gave a woman grief. She doesn't need you, too."

"I'm on an errand for Monsignor McNulty," Bohannon said. "What could be more benign that that?"

She eyed him skeptically. "It doesn't sound like you." She turned the key, the Cherokee's motor rumbled, she let go the parking brake, and started rolling the shiny machine out into the sunshine. She halted it. "You just go easy, now, you hear?" She glanced up at the deck above her. "She looks strong, but I've been a doctor for a long time, and I'd say any more weight on her shoulders, and she'll be down sick, too."

"Belle, it's nothing," Bohannon said. "Just a couple of questions. Only take a minute."

"You stick to that," she said, and backed down the pine-needly slope to the street. He started up the plank steps to the deck. She called out to him, "And don't get yourself hurt this time. I'm warning you. I'm booked solid till September." And she drove off.

The woman who came to the screen door looked big enough and strong enough to hurt him if she wanted to. Or to dig that grave, if that was what she wanted. She wasn't fat, but her bones were big, her shoulders square, and she stood five foot ten in flat-heeled shoes. A checkered green dishtowel was tied around her gray hair. Paint smeared her forehead, and she was rubbing paint from her big hands with a rag. The smell of paint was strong. She peered at him.

"I'm sorry," she said. "Do I know you?"

He told her who he was. "Something a little out of the way has happened up at the seminary. I thought I'd ask—"

"Monsignor McNulty was here only last week," she said. "He and my father are old friends. As scholars. My father is an atheist. They have lively arguments. Used to."

"I'm not here to see him, I'm here to see you."

"That's a surprise. I'm painting, and I have to get on with it." She pushed the screen open. "Will you come in?" She walked away through a dark living room that was lined with bookshelves. Magazines he took to be learned journals were stacked on a woolly carpet, on dusty tables, chairs, a worn sofa. He followed her into a room behind an open staircase that led up. "I've moved my files and word processor out of here. He's got to be downstairs, or he'll never try exercising." She bent to work a sheepskin roller in a pan of paint on a blue plastic drop cloth on the floor. "And I can feed him and tend to him down here easier too. Those stairs! Athletes aren't the only ones whose legs go first." She set the roller to the wall again. "What do you want?"

"Your father's an expert on this area, right?"

She sighed, laid the dry roller down in the pan, walked into the living room and pulled books from the shelves. An armload. She brought them to him. "Local Indians, customs, language, art, the first white settlers, the Santa Barbara mission, the one at San Luis Obispo, a biography of Father Serra. Definitive once. Now younger men have dug deeper."

"What about the mission that failed?" Bohannon gave her back the books. "Up where the seminary is now. Does he know a lot about that?"

"Everything there is to know." She carried the books away and put them back. "He spent years piecing together the crumbling old records. Even went to Spain to try to find more." She came back, threw him a wan smile, bent to soak the roller again, and stood to paint another section of wall. "He hated it when they built over the ruins in 1950. He loved those old broken walls, the bell tower."

"And the cemetery where the monks were buried?" Bohannon said. "Deserted now, just the gravestones and the oaks. He ever talk about that?"

She gave a nod. "He used to spend quiet times alone up there. He loved the peacefulness, away from the world."

"You do a lot of gardening, professor?"

The question startled her. She stared at him. "I have," she began sharply, and corrected herself, "I *had* a full-time academic career, Mr. Bohannon. I've never had time for hobbies. Or housework. That stopped when my mother died—years ago. And God knows, my father would never lift a finger. Selfish?" Her laugh was bitter. "You'd have to invent a new word."

A shout came from upstairs. "Bob, you bitch. What have you done with my medieval Latin dictionary? If it isn't in my hands in two minutes, I'll piss the bed for you."

"Excuse me," Roberta Thornbury said, and hurried off.

When she came back, flush-faced, Bohannon asked her, "I wondered if maybe you'd planted a tree lately?"

"Not I." She went at painting again, angry, splashing drops on herself. "But some students brought me a California pepper tree as a gift when I began this sabbatical. They set it in for me. You'll see it on your way out."

"A tree's an odd gift," Bohannon said.

"They want me to remember them," she said. "Go now, please."

Bohannon walked down the long living room to the sun-dazzled front door. "I hope your father gets better soon."

"He won't," she said. "He's dying. We have to face that."

The pepper tree was out there, all right, young and tenderly green, about five feet high. He hoped it would grow, but it looked as if it needed more sun. Poison oak had been chopped back here, and loose earth was scattered around. The tree had been planted lately, true, but how lately was anybody's guess.

The sleeping bag smelled of mildew when he dragged it down off the shelf of his bedroom closet. Along this stretch of coast it rained a lot, and what you did to prevent mildew was lay charcoal in drawers and closets, but there was a limit to how long a stick of charcoal would absorb damp, and he'd forgotten. He shouldered the bag, carried it along the pine plank hallway to the kitchen, took from the refrigerator a sack of sandwiches, filled a thermos with hot coffee, pulled from a drawer a three-cell flashlight. The Winchester was already in the truck. He put on his hat, pushed out into the slant of late afternoon sunlight, and knocked heels along the porch. Stubbs was out by the white rail gate, talking to two men on horseback. Bohannon made for the truck parked by the stables, and Stubbs hailed him.

"Hack? Come here, and meet the luckiest man in town."

Bohannon put his stuff into the truck, admired the Mercedes 450-SL parked beside it, walked to shake Timothy Powell's hand. He was a slender, light-skinned black, about twenty with a good smile. Bohannon asked him, "How does it feel?"

"A little scary," Powell said. "Nobody ever paid much attention to me before. Now they all want to be my friend. It's why I'm riding out now for an hour, just to be alone."

"Not quite alone." Bohannon looked at the other man. Something was wrong with his spine. There was a twist to it that gave the effect of shortening his upper body, and that pushed his right shoulder up in a hunch. He was in his thirties. Bohannon had seen him before. Where? The man held out a hand in a lightweight glove. Bohannon shook it.

"Dean Kirby," the man said, and smiled. "I'm manager of the supermarket. We don't want anything to happen to Tim. It's my assignment to keep him safe."

"Not his mother, this time?" Stubbs asked.

Powell laughed. "She treats me like I was ten years old, doesn't she? I'm lucky, but that just makes her more afraid."

"You've got steady horses there," Bohannon said. "You'll be all right. Congratulations again. Have a nice ride."

"Thank you," Powell said. "Goodnight."

It didn't start out like a good night. He worked for a time up the ladder in an oak, but while the stretching didn't bother him—his work around the stables kept him fit—his feet began to hurt soon from the ladder rungs. Also, he was missing some witch's broom because of the poor light. The flashlight beam cast too many shadows. And if you weren't thorough, if you missed any of the pesky parasites, the work was pointless. After an hour, he gave up, clambered down, rolled out the sleeping bag, sat on it, pulled off his boots. He lit a cigarette, drank coffee, and listened to the crickets. The view from here was of mountains sloping away below, shadow-creased under the moon. A window glowed in a canyon house far off—maybe his own, he couldn't be sure. Along a stretch of coast road moved the lonely lights of cars. Small neons colored the sky above Madrone. The pine-bristly black hills of Settlers Cove were sharp against the moonlit ocean. The coffee unsettled his gut. He rattled open the bag, and ate half a sandwich. Then he took the flashlight and patrolled the old cemetery. He wanted to be sure any watcher knew someone was here. In crossing the acre first from side to side, then up and down, he made it a point to stop at the empty grave and shine the light into it and all around it—three, four times. He wished the light would show him something. It showed him nothing. He went back to the sleeping bag and lay down.

Crackling twigs woke him. He hadn't meant to sleep, but he'd managed it anyway, hadn't he? "Who's that?" He sat up, groped with a numb hand for the flashlight, and shone it into the round, be-spectacled face of the lad who'd worked in the oak this morning. If he'd been given the boy's name, he'd forgotten it. The boy blinked in the beam of the flashlight and swallowed but didn't speak. Bohannon pushed to his feet. "What's on your mind? What are you doing up here?"

The boy moistened his lips. "I—have to talk to you."

"Talk away," Bohannon said, and gestured with the flashlight. The beam glinted on the barrel of the Winchester that leaned against the trunk of the oak that sheltered this spot.

"Is that a gun?" the pudgy boy said faintly.

"It seemed like a good idea," Bohannon said. "What's your name—I don't think I know. You're a student here, right?"

"Yes. Delbert May. I think you know my father. He's a public defender for the county."

"Yes. Fred. So you're his son?" Come to think of it, there was a strong resemblance. May was known by law enforcement officers and the courts as Fat Freddie, but he was a good man, and a crackerjack lawyer. "Going to be a priest. How does he take that? He's a maverick himself, a radical."

The boy smiled wanly. "He says no matter how misguided I may be, I'm still his son, and he loves me."

"What did you want to tell me?" Bohannon said.

"It's just that—well"—the pudgy boy crouched and picked up a stick and poked aimlessly at the ground with it—"Father McNulty isn't really a-ware"—Delbert dodged an embarrassed glance at Bohannon, and his glasses glinted in the yellow light—"of all that goes on. Among the students. Right?"

"I wondered if he was," Bohannon said.

"Sometimes terrible things happen," Delbert said.

"Not murder," Bohannon said. "You don't mean murder."

"I mean talk of it," Delbert said softly. "I heard them. Kelly Sangster and Scott Hughes. Kelly was my roommate. I'd been home for the weekend, came back Sunday night, and they were in my room, arguing. But not shouting, talking low, so I was almost in the room before I realized they were there. And I heard Scott say, 'If you tell him I'll kill you, Kelly. Before I let you destroy me, I'll kill you and bury you'."

"What did it mean?" Bohannon said.

"I don't know. They hardly knew each other. Scott came bursting out of the room. He didn't see me, but I saw him, and I never saw anyone so angry. He was white with rage. His face was all twisted up with it. He ran down the hall and down the stairs like a blind man."

"Sunday night," Bohannon said. "What happened Monday?"

"Kelly brooded, stayed in the room, didn't eat, didn't go to classes. That night, I heard him moaning. I switched on the lamp. He was on his knees, praying. I said 'Sorry,' and turned off the light. Next morning, he packed and left."

"And he didn't tell you why?"

"He mumbled something about trouble at home." Delbert looked around at the dark cemetery. "Did anyone come about the grave?"

"Do you think Scott Hughes dug it for Kelly Sangster?"

"It's not realistic, is it? But when you talked about murder this morning, I wondered. That's why I'm here now. Where are you going? You're not going to tell the monsignor!"

"I'm not," Bohannon said. "You are. Come on."

"Nobody likes trouble," Edwin Sangster said. A sturdy man in his mid-forties, in tweed jacket and wool slacks, he laid a brown manila envelope on the monsignor's desk. Sangster's son, Kelly, a thin, freckled boy with misery in his eyes, stood by him. On a leather couch against a panelled wall sat Scott Hughes, dark hair, dark brows, dark beard stubble. His eyes were angry. Edwin Sangster said, "No man should make trouble for another—but sometimes we have no choice."

It was ten past one in the morning. Bohannon leaned in the doorway of Monsignor McNulty's study. Delbert May, moon face pale, expression pathetic as a martyr's, stood across the room by a window. After he'd told McNulty what he'd told Bohannon, the monsignor had phoned the Sangster house in Atascadero. Then he'd sent Delbert to fetch a file folder from the next office, and to bring Hughes. Now everyone was here. McNulty sat back of his desk under a large wooden crucifix—Indian carving by the look of it, rough and cruel. With a solemn look, the old man closed the file folder.

Kelly Sangster said, "I wrestled with it for a long time."

The monsignor laid a briar pipe in a big brass ashtray, where it kept on smoldering, and pulled from the manila envelope a sheaf of Xerox copies of newspaper items. He studied these through heavy, horn-rimmed reading glasses, white hair shining in the lamplight, the only sound in the room the shuffling of the pages. He took the glasses off and looked gravely at the dark boy on the couch. "Have you seen these?"

Hughes nodded. "Kelly showed them to me."

"And the evildoer in these terrible accounts is you? The pictures appear most certainly to be of you." The old man waited but Hughes only looked away, mouth twitching sullenly. The monsignor said, "Where did you get the academic records in your file?"

"Bought them. From a student who worked in the office at Blair College. Stuck in my own photograph."

"Then somewhere there is a real Scott Hughes?"

"He died right after he graduated. Car crash. No good my denying it. I couldn't buy his fingerprints, could I?"

"So it was you"—McNulty held up the clippings—"who five years ago attacked this young couple in the dark, raped the girl, stole the car, and left the young man a cripple for life. You are"—he peered at the papers—"Earl Evan Gerber?"

"Not any more. I was a kid then. Sixteen. Out of control, mixed up, full of emotions I couldn't deal with. I'm not like that anymore, monsignor." He glared at Kelly Sangster. "It was just rotten luck he recognized me."

"Sometimes we make our luck," McNulty said. "If you'd come here honestly, as yourself, this needn't have happened."

The dark boy snorted. "Come on. The Fathers would have turned me down without a second thought. Rape? Mayhem? They wouldn't have cared that I'd served my time, I'd learned, I'd changed. They'd never have believed me."

"Stranger things have happened," McNulty said. "You never know till you try."

"I lied because I thought I had to," the dark boy

cried. "I wanted to become a priest—to make up for what I'd done. Scott Hughes had perfect credentials. As him, there'd be no chance I'd be turned down. I needed a break. I had to make that break for myself."

"Yes, yes." The old man gave him a weary smile. "Well, perhaps it can be sorted out." He glanced at a big, slow-ticking oak clock above the doorway. "We'll see, won't we? In the fullness of time."

"Maybe there's hope, Scott," Kelly Sangster said.

"Not because of you," the dark boy snarled. "I should have killed you when I had the chance." He lunged off the couch, knocked Edwin Sangster aside, clutched Kelly by the throat. Bohannon stepped in, pulled him off, twisted his arms up behind his back. The boy yelped and struggled. He was stocky and strong, but Bohannon was bigger, tougher, older. He looked at the monsignor.

"Phone the sheriff," he said. "Calm down, Earl, or I'll break your arms. That's better. Deep breaths. That's it." Delbert May was staring, open-mouthed, wide-eyed. Kelly was holding his own throat, gulping, in trouble with trying to breathe. His father had his arms around him and kept asking him if he was all right. Bohannon said to Earl Evan Gerber, "How long did it take you to dig that grave all by yourself? It's a big job."

"What? What?" Gerber struggled. "Let me go. What the hell are you talking about?"

The monsignor dialed the telephone. Shakily.

Bohannon said to Gerber, "You told Kelly you'd bury him. There's a new grave up in the old friar's cemetery."

118

"Not me," Gerber said. "I didn't do it. I swear."

Bohannon looked at Gerber's hands. The skin was unmarred. They were not workman's hands, so there should have been blisters. There were no blisters. Bohannon was going to have to spend the rest of the night up in that graveyard.

Bohannon got out of the truck with the grocery list in his hand. Bright plastic pennons fluttered over the shopping center parking lot, where cars waited, gleaming in sunlight. A section of lot near the supermarket had been blocked off by wooden barricades. A portable platform, plywood painted green, stood not far from the market's glass doors. A steel-legged table stood on the platform, and on the stiff green cloth that covered the table was arrayed glittering new merchandise, watches, stereos, television sets, microwaves, toaster ovens. A new light motorcycle gleamed red at one end of the table, a ten-speed bike at the other. In front of the platform was parked a shiny yellow Japanese hatchback with a big blue satin bow stuck to its top. A banner fluttered on the front of the market above the doors— SAVE-MORE'S GREAT SUMMER GIVEAWAY. Bohannon had forgotten all about it.

A young woman and two young men climbed onto the platform now. The girl and one of the boys held electric guitars, and the other boy, a stubby one, held a Fender bass. They wore satin outfits stitched with glitter, blue, green, rose-red, and white cowboy hats, and white cowboy boots and little white neckerchiefs. They stood at microphones, smiled ruthlessly, and sang country western hits to listeners seated on steel folding chairs on the blacktop and, since the volume on their loudspeakers was turned up high, to half of Morro Bay as well, Bohannon thought.

The chairs were all full. Highschoolers and collegians were there in bikinis and surfer trunks. Young women with babies and toddlers. Old folks in straw hats, women mostly. Almost all Anglos. A few Latinos. A few Asians. No blacks. Wrong. In the front row—one slender, beautifully groomed woman. Dean Kirby, the market manager, leaned over her. They seemed to be talking urgently. Bohannon looked around for Tim Powell. Nowhere. Maybe they were keeping him inside the store, under wraps, until his big moment. If so, his mother, if that was who the woman was, seemed not to like it. Bohannon stepped past the barricades and went to her. The only empty chair was next to her, and he sat on it.

"That's for my son," she said. "I'm sorry."

"I thought it was," Bohannon said. "Where is he?"

"We came together," she said, "but he's strayed off someplace. Mr. Kirby can't find him. It's very upsetting. Who are you?"

Bohannon told her. Her face lit up.

"Ah, he loves to ride your horses," she said. "I'm so glad we found the place we did to live. It's only a mile up the canyon from you, you know. Opposite the seminary."

"New place," Bohannon said. "The family that built it—he was an engineer at the Diablo plant. Got transferred."

She nodded. "It's comfortable. Away from people. That's what we both wanted. I sold my duplex in L.A. to buy it. You see, it's worth a black boy's life to stay in the city. Murder is the chief cause of death among urban black men age sixteen to twenty-four—did you know that?"

"I didn't know that," Bohannon said.

"And there's drugs and there's gangs, all manner of dangers. I didn't want that for Timothy. He was spared to me, you understand. I had four beautiful children. There was a fire. He was the only one got out alive."

"Was that why he told me he was lucky?"

"It was long ago," she said, "when he was very small."

"Well, he's been lucky again," Bohannon said, and nodded at the platform. Just then, from behind it, balloons rose in a rush straight up into the sky. The people on the chairs gasped, cheered, laughed, and shielded their eyes with their hands to watch the balloons against the sun—they were green and white. There must have been a hundred of them. Bohannon said, "Maybe he'll buy a horse of his own now."

"He could," she said, watching the balloons. "Aren't they pretty?" And then, fretfully, "Where can he be? Where can that Timothy be?"

"He'll turn up," Bohannon said. "He wouldn't want to miss his fifty thousand dollars. Nobody would."

But he missed it. The band gave up the microphones to Dean Kirby and two assistant managers dressed in green jackets and white cotton gloves as Kirby was. They read names from cards, people struggled out of the rows of chairs and came forward to accept their prizes and tote them away. The crowd laughed and clapped. The giveaway started with the small prizes and worked up through the bicycle and the cruise tickets to the motorbike. At last, much of the crowd circled the yellow car and the lucky, sunburned, middle-aged lemon ranchers who had won it. The stringy man in whipcords raised the bright keys and jingled them above his head, and grinned all around him with tobacco-stained teeth. Then the car rolled away, and it was time for the Grand Prize. But when Kirby announced his name, and looked eagerly around the crowd, Tim Powell did not come to the platform. Kirby blinked at Mrs. Powell, eyebrows raised. He appeared puzzled to see Bohannon in the chair beside her.

"I guess he must be crowd-shy." Kirby laughed, and the people on the folding chairs laughed with him, murmured among themselves, craned their necks to see. Kirby said, "Must have developed stage fright." He bent close to the microphone. "Come on, Tim Powell." He raised the envelope and waved it. "There's fifty thousand beautiful bucks in here, my man, and all for you. Where are you, Tim Powell?"

But in the end he had to give the check to Powell's mother. She smiled for the local television team—a frizzy-haired blond young woman with a microphone, and a pot-bellied man with a camera on his shoulder—but when she returned to her place, she looked worried. Bohannon said, "I'll look around for your son, if you want me to. Is Kirby right? Is he shy? Maybe he's waiting in the car."

He wasn't waiting in the car. Mrs. Powell looked

bleakly at Bohannon. "No, he isn't shy. He wouldn't disappoint people, either, that nice Mr. Kirby, all those folks waiting to see him, the television." She turned to look at the departing people, the white-aproned box-boys folding up the clattering chairs, the moving cars. "Something's wrong, Mr. Bohannon. Oh, I was afraid of this. All that money." She pushed the envelope almost angrily into her shoulder bag. She looked into his eyes. "Yes, please, I'd be obliged. Find him for me if you can." The car keys were in her gloved fingers, but she made no move with them. He took them gently from her, and opened the car door for her. Sunbaked air came out. "Thank you." She sat herself behind the steering wheel.

"Here's my card," Bohannon said. "Phone me if he turns up. Maybe he got a ride home. With a friend."

"We haven't made any friends up here yet." She closed the car door, moved a switch to lower the window. "He won't enroll at the college until fall." She studied the card for a moment, tucked it into her purse, laid the purse on the seat next to her. "I hope I'm worried about nothing." She tried for a light laugh. "He always says I worry too much."

"They'll take a message at my place if I'm still out," Bohannon said. "And I'll phone you anyway, when I get there. Maybe I'll have him with me."

"I hope so." She started the car. "I'll bank this money first, then go straight home. That's where I'll be." She drove the car cautiously away among the others rolling slowly out of the shopping center.

He walked the cement verge, checking out all the businesses on the square—beauty parlor, camera shop, donut store, laundromat, dry cleaners, baby shop, party supplies, leather goods—he stayed there an extra minute, breathing in the rich smells—and finally the savings and loan at the corner. Lines at the tellers' windows had shortened, now that the lunch hour was over. Tim Powell wasn't there. But as he turned to leave, Bohannon remembered that it was here where he'd seen Kirby before. Yes, at the supermarket, sure. But in here, just last week, when Bohannon had been waiting to make a deposit in the stable's account, he'd seen Kirby over there, at a loan officer's desk. Arguing, wiping sweat off his forehead.

Bohannon did a circuit of the supermarket aisles. It wasn't likely Powell would choose the market to hide in, but it was worth a try. Bohannon found a young clerk in a green apron crouching beside a stack of cartons, using a rubber stamp machine to price canned soups. When Bohannon asked him for Dean Kirby, the answer was that Kirby had gone home early. Did Bohannon want to speak to the assistant manager? Bohannon said, "No, thanks," and left.

He drove to the waterfront, where white wooden decks and stairs took him past restaurants and boutiques that looked out on the blue bay, the great rock towering out of it, and white boats tilting and bobbing around the rock under bright orange, yellow, blue, green sails. He sat on a stool at an outdoor counter and with a bottle of Anchor beer washed down pita bread stuffed with a shrimp concoction. Against the glare, he looked at all the boats. Powell hadn't gone sailing.

He drove back to the supermarket, loaded a shiny wire cart with every item Stubbs had listed, and a few extras of his own, loaded the sacks into the truck, then found a pay phone. The phone often rang a long time at the stables. You could get tangled up far away when there were horses to look after. Like kids, you never knew what they'd think up to do. At last, Rivera answered, panting. Bohannon said, "Did Tim Powell show up to ride today? Did he want to be alone again?"

"He did not," Rivera said, "but his mother is here. She is waiting for you, Hack. She is very upset."

Rivera had a sense of fitness. The living room almost never got used, but this was where he had put Mrs. Powell. It, too, was a pine plank room with the pitched roof showing above rafters. There was a stone fireplace, Stubbs's rodeo trophies on the mantle, the Winchester racked above them. The furniture was covered in chintz to match the ruffled window curtains. Chintz wasn't Bohannon's choice but his wife's. A kidnapping and rape had cost Linda her sanity. She was in a hospital. It looked like she was never coming back, but Bohannon didn't change the chintz. Filled bookshelves occupied a wall. Oval braided rugs lay on floorboards Rivera kept polished. When Bohannon came in, Mrs. Powell got quickly to her feet.

"Oh, thank God," she said shakily. "You're here." She hadn't changed from her festive clothes. She pulled a rumpled paper from her shoulder bag and thrust it at him. "Look. Look what I found pushed under my front door when I got home."

Bohannon unfolded the paper. Letters cut from advertising flyers had been pasted to it to form words. I HAVE YOUR SON. IF YOU WANT TO SEE HIM ALIVE AGAIN GET ME 50 THOUSAND CASH. I WILL TELEPHONE INSTRUCTIONS. DO NOT TELL POLICE OR I WILL KILL HIM. BELIEVE ME.

"What shall I do?" she said.

"Go to the sheriff," Bohannon said.

"No," she said, "I can't risk Tim. He's all I've got."

"All right—then do as the man says." Bohannon looked at his watch. "Get the money from the bank, go home, and wait for him to call you."

She looked stricken. "Aren't you going to help me?"

"I'm going to try." Bohannon folded the paper, pushed it into a hip pocket. "I'll send Rivera with a gun to guard you. I have to get moving. I've only got till nightfall."

"What are you talking about?" she cried.

He was talking about that unused grave, but he didn't tell her so. He took the Winchester down from above the fireplace, and hurried her outdoors. "Rivera?" he shouted. He told Mrs. Powell, "The bank will close soon. Don't be late."

"What if he telephones?" She sounded frantic.

"I'll keep calling you to find out," Bohannon said.

He drove the old pickup down the canyon breakneck. It clattered and banged. The road was narrow, its blacktop old, grey, potholed, ragged at the edges. At one sharp corner, a squealing tire caught on one of those ragged edges, and nearly pitched him down a ravine of rocks and dry brush. He wrestled with the wheel, with the shift lever, with brakes and clutch. The truck went veering across to the other side, half climbed a cliff, nearly fell over, then rolled backward. He sat there for a minute, trying to collect himself. He was racing against time he probably didn't even have. That grave meant only one thing. The kidnapper had never meant to leave Tim Powell alive. Maybe it even meant the boy was already dead, was dead from the minute he was taken at the supermarket. But it was no good thinking that. If he was alive, maybe Bohannon could save him. He had to try. He yanked the truck into gear and headed down the road again.

The young woman's hair bushed out, red as a clown's wig. She had a long, sad nose. She fiddled with the flowers in a vase on her desk. "I'm sorry," she said, "but really, loan applications are confidential, Mr."—she peered at his card—"Bohannon. Who would trust us if they thought we discussed their financial problems with strangers?"

"It's a matter of saving a young man's life."

"Then why are you asking? Why not the sheriff?"

Bohannon pushed up out of the soft barrel chair, and jogged out of the place. He yanked the truck door open, clambered up inside, slammed the door. His head ached. He rubbed the back of his neck, twisted the key in the ignition, thumbed the starter button. He'd wanted a motive. He disliked guesswork. But he could go with his instincts. He had no choice. The motor caught. He let the handbrake go. Someone shouted his name. He stopped backing the truck and waited. A thin young black woman he'd noticed listening in the savings and loan office came running to him.

"He wanted the loan," she panted, "because his

wife has left him. She worked. That gave them enough income to make the house payments. He can't do it alone. But we can't help. A third mortgage—he'd never manage it."

"Thank you," Bohannon said. "Much obliged."

"That Miss Dempsey"—the young woman blinked angrily—"she's so high and mighty."

"It takes all kinds," Bohannon said. "I like yours better."

The old man and his son and his sister's son were not in the Mexican graveyard today. People in their best clothes knelt around a flower-margined grave while the wind flapped the robes of the priest who read the service, and gulls circled overhead. Bohannon looked in a dusty side mirror, found the road empty, and swung the truck around. The place he was looking for, without quite knowing it, was called *La Cantina*. The name flaked off grimy white stucco on a corner. He found a parking place and walked back to it. Mariachi music met him as he pushed aside a greasy curtain inside the door. A bar stretched along one side of the room, a few tables were scattered along the other. A short hall at the end of the room led to another room where a pool table stood under a green shaded hanging lamp.

The air was thick with cigarette smoke and the smell of spilled beer. Men, young and old, leaned along the bar, straw hats pushed back on their heads. Laughter and arguments were loud above the music, which blared from a juke box, most of whose internal lights had died of old age. Bohannon leaned on the bar, waiting to accustom his eyes to the dark after the glare of sunlight outside. He asked for Dos Equis and got a bottle with another label altogether, and a wet glass. He paid for it, filled the glass, drank from it, lit a cigarette. When he had finished the beer and the smoke, he went along the room and through the hallway that smelled of washroom disinfectant. Jose and Raymondo were not playing pool, but they were watching others play, a man with a big belly and a skeletal man, both in cotton plaid shirts.

Bohannon stood beside Jose, the muscular son of the old gravedigger. Jose paid him no attention. The set-up of colored balls on the green table was complicated. He wanted to see what the big-bellied man would do about it. Raymondo watched with the same concentration. Bohannon said, "You dug that grave up behind the seminary, didn't you? Only you were afraid to admit it in front of your father. You didn't want him to know you had earned money you didn't give him."

Jose grabbed Raymondo's arm and started out of the room. Bohannon stepped in front of them. "I won't tell your father. Who was it who hired you?"

"We know nothing, *señor*," Jose said. "We must go, now."

"Stay a minute. The one who hired you did not have you do the work to no purpose. He is going to kill a young man and put him into that grave."

Raymondo's eyes widened. "He said nothing of this."

"Be quiet," Jose told him sharply. "You are a fool."

"So, you did dig the grave," Bohannon said.

Raymondo was a pasty color. He looked ready to faint.

"No, no, *señor*. We did not. Yes, he came and asked us to do it, but we refused."

"Describe the man for me," Bohannon said.

Jose stuck out his jaw. "We can say nothing."

"Not to prevent a murder?" Bohannon said.

"He paid us fifty dollars to forget him," Raymondo said. "To say nothing of what he had asked us to do."

"What are you," Jose yelled at him, "that your mouth goes so incessantly? A woman?"

"It's all right," Bohannon said. "I won't tell anyone."

The telephone against the side of the building didn't work. Bohannon trudged back to the truck, the downing sun in his eyes. The sun glared on the dusty windshield when he got behind the steering wheel. He looked at his watch. He had driven far and wide this afternoon. Time was running out on him. Daylight was running out. He headed back toward Morro Bay, Madrone, Rodd Canyon. He pulled in at a highway filling station for gas and a swipe at the windshield, and here the telephone worked. Mrs. Powell answered shrilly.

"It's Hack Bohannon," he said. "Did the call come?"

"Yes. He said to put the money in a supermarket sack and leave it under the broken adobe wall on the west side of that old burial ground up behind the seminary."

"Did you talk to Tim?" Bohannon said.

"I asked to," she said, "but he refused."

Bohannon felt cold in his gut. "Did he put a time to your delivering the ransom?"

"He said to do it now," she said, "but I've been waiting for your call. That's what Manuel felt we should do. Perhaps that's right, but I'm anxious to have Tim back. I want to hold him in my arms."

"Did you recognize the caller's voice?" Bohannon said.

"I—don't think so, no." She asked sharply, "Why? Should I have? Do you know who he is, Mr. Bohannon?"

"A man who wears gloves," Bohannon said, "to hide the blisters on his hands. Let me talk to Manuel, please."

Rivera took the receiver. Bohannon said, "No matter how frantic she gets, don't let her deliver that money."

"What are you saying?" Rivera said.

"That the kidnapper is the one who dug that grave," Bohannon said. "He never meant to turn Tim over. He meant to kill him, from the start."

"*Madre de Dios,*" Rivera breathed.

"Maybe he already has," Bohannon said. "But once he gets the money, there won't be any maybe about it."

"But why?" Rivera said.

"He has no choice," Bohannon said. "Tim knows who he is."

It was a handsome new house, set on the ridge a mile past the seminary, and with a glorious view, clear to the sea. The garage was at road level, the redwood door shut down and padlocked. Bohannon got out of the truck, feeling naked. The only gun he owned was the Winchester, and Rivera had that. Rivera had to have it. The man could come to the Powell house for the money. Bohannon dragged a tire iron from under the seat of the truck, walked to the garage door, snapped open the padlock. He raised the door. There stood the new Mercedes 450-SL, all twenty thousand dollars worth. The owner was still here. Good. Bohannon walked to a workbench at the rear of the garage. Under it he found what he expected—mattock, spade, long-handled shovel, new, all of them, blades clotted with dirt. And bits of witch's broom. Blood was on the handle of the shovel. Those blisters had broken, hadn't they?

A set of redwood steps with two-by-four rails went zig zag up the slope to the house. Bohannon climbed them softly as he could, not letting the worn heels of his boots sound. Crowding trees shadowed the steps. In their cold shadows, he shivered. He clutched the tire iron tightly. Curtains were drawn across wide windows that faced the deck. He stepped quietly onto the deck and spent a minute on the view. It had cost a fortune by itself, he reckoned. Out to sea, the sun was a flattened red fireball on the horizon. He tried the knob of the carved front door. The door was locked. He moved tiptoe along a side deck, where he found French doors that were not locked. He opened one, waited, stepped cautiously inside.

The room was large and handsome. He knew little about such things, but he judged the thick carpet underfoot, glowing with dark reds rich as stained glass, was oriental—the real thing. A clock of brass and glass on the mantle of a broad brick fireplace had *Cartier* on its face. Built into a side wall a forty-inch television set read Mitsubishi. He guessed that cost a bundle. He didn't recall ever having heard the brand names on the stereo equipment—receiver, cassette deck, compact disk player. He did know the names on the bottles behind the bar—Glenlivet, Wild Turkey, Beefeater. Only the best for Dean Kirby. If he had to kill for it.

Bohannon heard a voice. It came from the rear of the house somewhere. Not clearly. He couldn't make out words. Then a door opened. And he knew the voice for Kirby's. He sounded tense and angry. "I can kill you here, if you like. And drag you down the stairs to the car. It's all the same to me. If twenty more minutes of living don't mean anything to you, I'll just pull this trigger now. Ah. That's better." Bohannon heard stumbling footsteps. He heard a human sound to go with them. Maybe the human who made it was Tim Powell. Bohannon ducked behind the bar and crouched down there, between a small, humming refrigerator and rows of shiny glasses of all shapes and sizes on shelves under the bar. There was a hint of expensive perfume. A memory of Mrs. Dean Kirby.

He couldn't see from here, but he heard the shoes of Kirby and his prisoner stumble into the room. And pass the bar. He stood up slowly. Kirby's back was to him. A revolver in one hand, pressed into Tim Powell's back, Kirby was turning the deadbolt on the front door. Bohannon stepped soundlessly from behind the bar, and flung the tire iron at the fireplace. It clanged. Kirby jerked toward the sound, and fired the gun. The beautiful clock shattered. Kirby stared at it as if his heart would break. Bohannon tackled him. Kirby fell back against the door. His head struck it hard. He slumped down, eyes shut, shoulders against the door, one leg folded awkwardly under him. The gun slipped from his bandaged fingers. Bohannon picked it up. Tim Powell was staring at him. A wide band of adhesive tape was across his mouth. Bohannon pulled this off.

"Thank God," Powell said. "That man is crazy. Locked me in the market freezer while he passed out the prizes. Then dragged me here to wait till it's dark so he can kill me and bury me. Did you know that?"

"It took me a while to figure it out," Bohannon said. "Sorry about that. Turn around—I'll untie your hands. We'll phone the sheriff. Then we'll take you home to your mother. She wants to hold you in her arms."

"I don't know why she worries so much." Tim Powell rubbed his wrists. "I keep telling her I'm lucky."

"I guess you are, at that," Bohannon said.

Merely Players

What had wakened him? He lay in the dark, listening to the scree of crickets out in the cool canyon night. Their chirping had a slow, sleepy rhythm. He turned over and saw the curtains move in the breeze that came up the canyon from the ocean, bringing the smell of sage and eucalyptus. Fifty yards off in the stables a horse nickered softly and set down a heavy hoof in its box stall. Horses were his business. He kept his own for strangers to ride, and he boarded horses for owners with no place to keep them. He listened carefully in case there was trouble. It didn't sound that way. He grunted, turned over, started to drift off again when he heard footfalls, soft ones on the white gravel beyond the long plank porch that fronted the board-and-batten ranch house.

He got out of bed, went to the window, pushed the curtain aside, peered out. Outdoor lighting shone on the stables at night, and some of its reflection reached here, and he thought he saw a big man standing out there staring at the house. He thought he knew the man. He pulled a cambric shirt off the ladderback of a chair, flapped into it, kicked into worn jeans. His watch lay on the chair seat. He strapped this on, and legged out the window onto the porch. "Something I can do for you?" He read the watch. Early. Nine-twenty. "Mitch Russell, isn't it? From the Coach & Four?"

"Can I talk to you?" Russell took a step closer. "I know it's late. I'm sorry. But I can't think of anyplace else." He smelled of whiskey. "I need help."

Bohannon sighed to himself. It was often this way. He wished it wasn't. He loved horses and the life he lived here. Human beings he wasn't that keen about. But he'd been a decent sheriff's deputy for fourteen years, and though he'd retired, people wouldn't forget it. He became a last refuge. So he took out a private investigator's license. There seemed no way around it.

"Come on," he said, and moved along the porch, the boards dry, cold, gritty under his bare soles. He pulled open the aluminum screen door to the kitchen, unlocked the wooden door, pushed it open, switched on a low-key lamp in the middle of the big, deal table in the center of the pine plank room. Around it cupboards loomed, a giant cookstove, a big old icebox. Russell followed him into the place and stood. Bohannon lit a burner on the stove, filled a tall blue enamel coffee pot with water at the sink, set it on the burner to heat, got down coffee from a cupboard. "Sit down," he said. "We'll have coffee in a few minutes." He went to the table and pulled out a chair for himself and lit a cigarette. "What's happened?"

"Eugenia's dead," Russell said. "My wife. Somebody shot her." Behind his ruddy beard and mustache and the blue granny glasses he always wore, Mitch Russell was a handsome man, and in the quiet lamplight he looked younger than Bohannon had gauged him to be. "When I got home from the pub at six-twenty, she was lying on the floor." His voice wobbled for a second. He swallowed hard. "By the fireplace. Navajo rug there. It got blood on it. She'd hate that."

"She didn't shoot herself?" Bohannon said.

Russell winced, then gave his head a quick shake. "There's no gun. And it wasn't robbery. Nothing's stolen." He wore a ruffled white shirt and black string tie, black trousers, polished black shoes. He was a publican. The Coach & Four was supposed to be nineteenth century English. All glossy oak and brass and pewter, it was one of many fancy shops that had opened in Madrone in late years, to catch the tourists taking Highway One up the coast to Monterey and Big Sur—eateries, antique shops, gifts, fancy groceries. Overpriced, all of them. A beer and sandwich in the Coach & Four cost ten bucks. Bohannon never ate or drank there unless on business. Mitch Russell and his handsome blonde goddess wife, Eugenia, fit right in. "Shot her and ran away. Why?"

"Burglary in progress," Bohannon guessed, "and she surprised him. You didn't call the sheriff. You sat down with a bottle and tried to sort it out, and thought of me?"

"The sheriff would lock me up," Russell said.

"Why?" Bohannon said. "Did you kill her?"

"No. But I'm not Mitch Russell. I'm Avery Ames." He waited a moment for a sign that Bohannon knew the name. Bohannon didn't. "I was an actor. Daytime soaps. I wasn't famous, and the pay wasn't much. But I married a rich woman. This was six years ago, seven. She owned a big power boat. We used it a lot. Then, one weekend she dropped overboard when I was below. She drowned. Her body washed up on the beach at Malibu a few days later. They said I killed her for her money. I served five years for manslaughter. When I got out, Eugenia was waiting for me. We married, I put on weight, grew a beard, we moved up here."

"And lived quietly under a false name," Bohannon said.

"And now somebody's murdered Eugenia," Russell said. "And you know how that's going to go. I'll be back in San Quentin again. I can't cut it, Bohannon. This time, they'll kill me. They're not human beings in there."

"So what do you think I can do?" Bohannon said.

"Find out who killed her," Russell said. "I'll pay you well." His face flushed in the lamplight. He was talking about his wife's money. Everyone knew Eugenia Russell was rich, and some said she kept the handsome Mitch as her fancy boy. She was older than he, that was certain. "Could I have a drink?" He looked around at the looming shadows.

"I'll get the coffee," Bohannon said. "You need a clear head. So do I." He went to the stove. When he came back to the table, he set a thick mug in front of Russell and another at his own place. Russell was smoking and looked sulky. "While I'm finding the one who killed her," Bohannon asked, and sat down, "what will you be doing?"

"Hiding out," Russell said. "What else can I do? I'll be the first one the police will suspect."

"Sheriff," Bohannon corrected him, and lit a cigarette for himself. "It won't do. You're innocent. Go direct to the sheriff and tell him all about it, including who you are. You're not in any trouble. Don't put yourself there."

Russell grunted and tried the hot coffee.

Bohannon said, "Who do you think killed her?"

Russell shook his head. "I don't know. I've thought and thought. All I draw is blanks."

"What would the reason be?" Bohannon said.

"I'm the only one with any reason." Russell turned ash off his cigarette by rubbing it in the big, old, square glass ashtray on the table. "I mean, that's how law enforcement will see it." He looked up sharply, the blue glasses glinting. "We'd been having arguments lately, Eugenia and I. Sometimes in private, but sometimes in the pub, where people heard us. She got along with everybody else, got along fine. You knew her. Sunny and good-natured as all get out. Everybody liked her. It sounds wrong to call her a good Joe. She had too much class for that. But that's what she was, right?"

"A charmer." Bohannon nodded. "She'll be missed."

"Tell me about it," Russell said bleakly. "Christ, what a mess. Sometimes it's hard not to be superstitious. When a thing like this happens to you twice?"

"Arguments about what?" Bohannon drank coffee and watched the copper-bearded man.

"About the theatre. She wanted me to close it."

It was in a long room behind the pub. Russell had only opened it last year. A community playhouse. A lot of retired people with time on their hands lived in and around Madrone. Acting in plays was a way to use time, to liven up too many sunny, empty days, too many snug evenings by crackling fires, dreams come true that weren't as sweet in actuality as they had seemed when you had to go to a job every day. Those who didn't act in the plays or help out painting sets or sewing costumes went to watch their neighbors perform. Bohannon had gone once. With T. Hodges, a young female sheriff's officer he'd taken a shine to. He hadn't gone again. He had no tolerance for amateurs. What was the point in doing things badly? Better not to do them at all.

"You started it because you missed acting," he said.

"She didn't know how much of me it was going to use up." Russell put out his cigarette, drank some more coffee. "She wanted more for herself." He grimaced. "I kept promising—but we had less and less time together. So she said I had to close it up." His laugh was short and humorless. "She had the right. It was her money, wasn't it?"

Bohannon pushed back his chair and rose.

"Where you going?" Russell scowled.

"We're both going." Bohannon went and turned off the burner under the coffee pot. "Down to the sheriff's. I have a friend there. I'll put in a word for you. You'll be okay."

"I don't think so." Russell sat where he was.

"How can I find who killed your wife?" Bohannon said. "You don't give me any leads. The sheriff's men can do it."

"I'll sit in a cell," Russell said. "You'll see."

"You're over-reacting." Bohannon moved to the door. His sweaty old Stetson hung from a brass hook there. He took the hat down and put it on. Boots stood on the floor. He sat on a straight, flower-painted Mexican chair with a straw seat, and pulled the boots on. They smelled of the stable. "Come on. Let's get it over with. You can stop being afraid then. That will feel good."

Russell got wearily to his feet. "She'll still be dead."

"That's another thing." Bohannon pulled open the door. "You can't leave her lying there. It's been too long already."

Russell looked at him glumly. "Damn," he said. "Damn."

"What the hell happened to you?"

Gerard stared at him from the far side of a desk strewn with papers, file folders, photographs. The night shift was usually quiet in the sheriff's substation. But it still smelled as it had always smelled, and Bohannon hated the smell, hated the way the light fell in the halls, the offices. Two bad things had happened to him at the end of his time as a peace officer here. He couldn't forget them or forgive them. One had ended in the whitewash of an officer he knew had shot dead an unarmed Latino boy at a teenage dust-up on Saturday night in Cayucos. The other, involving heroin smugglers on a grimy, stinking fishing boat up from Mexico, had ended in the kidnap, beating, gang rape of Linda, his wife. Her body had recovered, but not her mind. She was in a mental hospital—it looked like forever. Bohannon had left the department then. He never enjoyed coming back here, but sometimes there was no way around it. This was one of those times.

"I look worse than I feel," he said. His shirt was

ripped, one sleeve almost off. His jeans were torn at the knee. He'd lost his hat. There figured to be dry grass in his hair. He had bled from scrapes and scratches. "I was bringing Mitch Russell down here to talk to you. He didn't want to come. I misjudged how badly he didn't want to come." Bohannon lowered himself, wincing, onto a straight chair. He was bruised all over. "A mile above town, he asked me to stop so he could get out and tend to nature. Made a ruckus out in the brush, called me to help him, like a fool I went. And he hit me from behind, threw me down a gully, went off with the truck."

"He's a big guy," Gerard said, "but I never took him for violent. Kind of artsy-craftsy, wouldn't you say?"

"Not anymore," Bohannon said. "His wife is dead, murdered. He found the body. He came to me instead of calling you because he thought you'd lock him up for killing her."

"Why would I do that?" Gerard said. "Did he kill her?"

"I don't think so." Then Bohannon explained the why of it. Gerard's eyebrows went up and stayed up until Bohannon finished the explanation. Then Gerard picked up the telephone. Bohannon went to the washroom and cleaned himself up. When he came back, Gerard was on his feet, heading out the door to the parking lot, under its tall, rustling eucalyptus trees. "I put out an APB. I'm on my way to the Russell place. You well enough to come along?"

"No," Bohannon said, "but I'm coming anyway."

The patrol car swung with a squeal of worn tires off the highway and followed jittering headlight beams along the crooked trails among the tall pines in the hills of Settlers Cove. Gerard said, "I remember the Avery Ames case. He would have got off, but before she drowned he'd taken to signing her name to checks without asking her first."

Bohannon grunted. He glimpsed through the windshield a crossroads sign as the headlights touched it. "This is the road. Cholmondeley." He pronounced it Chumley. Gerard spun the steering wheel and glanced at him. "Is that how you say it? Jesus, I've been wrestling with all those syllables for years. Chumley? No kidding?"

The road climbed steeply. The worn gears of the county car labored. When the road levelled off, they saw ahead the winking, turning, amber light on the top of an ambulance. A new Cherokee wagon stood beside it. So did another county car whose headlights shone into ferns, poison oak, tree trunks. Gerard let his car lurch half into the roadside ditch, killed the engine, and got out. Bohannon got out painfully on the ditch side. A young uniformed officer came toward them.

"She in there?" Gerard said.

"Way you reported it—dead," the young officer said.

"That you, Belle?" Gerard called, and a woman in a Levis outfit waved an arm. For a second the ambulance light touched her white hair. Gerard, the young officer, and Bohannon walked to where she stood at the foot of redwood stairs that climbed high to a house where all the windows glared yellow through the pines. Belle Hesseltine said, "You brought Hack, too." She eyed Bohannon. "Had to beat him up, first, did you?"

"He arrived at my office like that," Gerard said.

"Mitch Russell did it to me," Bohannon told her.

"Looks like his day for misbehaving," the old doctor said. "Shot his wife in the throat. Killed her instantly. The bullet's not in the body. Went through and hit the fireplace, I'd judge. I didn't find it, but it should be there. You'll locate it, I expect. Small caliber."

"Big enough to kill her," Bohannon said.

"You finished with the body?" Gerard said.

"Something wrong?" she said.

"You were supposed to wait till I said go."

"Waste of time," she said. "I live just around the bend. Lieutenant, I'm only filling in for the medical examiner. I don't know the rules. But I didn't disturb anything. She's just the way I found her. What got into Mitch? Sweet man, I always thought, spineless but sweet."

"I don't think he did it," Bohannon said.

"And that's why he beat you up?" Belle Hesseltine said. "All right. Not my problem." She picked up her kit and turned away. "I'm going home, unplug my telephone, and get a night's sleep, for a change." She walked toward her shiny Cherokee, straight and brisk as a young girl.

"What was the time of death?" Gerard called.

"I'll know better tomorrow, when I check the stomach contents." She lifted her kit through a window into the car. "But by the body temperature, it was someplace between three this afternoon"—she walked out of sight behind the tall car that was a box of darkness where it stood—"and sundown."

144

A door opened, springs squeaked, the door slammed, and the lights of the Cherokee glared on the ambulance. She started the engine, let go the handbrake. "Good night," she called, and drove off into the night.

"No way to face her down," Gerard said. "Even when she's wrong, she's right. I can't wait to get old."

On the deck at the top of the steps, lighted from the rear by the glare from the house, a red-haired fat boy in green tunic and waist-tied green pants, and a hollow-cheeked brown boy in the same kind of outfit were smoking cigarettes. They had unfolded a gurney just inside the sliding glass door panels of the house. A folded green blanket lay on the gurney. The red-haired fat boy said:

"When can we take the body, Lieutenant?"

"You got a lot of calls on your time tonight?" Gerard asked. "Bodies littering the landscape, are they?"

"No, sir," the fat boy said. "Nothing like that."

"I didn't think so," Gerard said and led Bohannon into the Russell living room, stepping around the gurney. The young deputy followed them. Eugenia Russell lay as her husband had said, on a Navajo rug in front of a handsome fireplace. She did not, as it often said in books, appear to be asleep. Her eyes were open, and that her mouth hung open gave her a look of surprise. She wasn't surprised. Not anymore. She was dressed in beige cotton trousers and jacket, expensive, cut large and blowsy, the way young women dressed these days, though Eugenia hadn't been exactly young. Her shirt had broad pink stripes, to match her high-heeled sandals. One sandal had a broken heel, not quite detached.

"See that?" Gerard had crouched beside her. "She must have stepped backward too fast. When she saw the gun."

"I guess so." Bohannon bent and picked the bullet out of the ashes in the firebasket. A clean chip out of the sooty stones lining the fireplace showed where the bullet had struck and bounced off. It was a bunged-up lump of lead—thirty-two caliber, he thought. Gerard was busy with Eugenia Russell's pockets. Bohannon looked at the young deputy. He said, "No luck finding the gun?"

"It's not in the house." The boy's mind seemed elsewhere. He kept checking his watch. "Should I get my flashlight and look around outdoors? By the deck, by the stairs?"

"Go ahead," Gerard said, without looking up. "Only be careful of the poison oak."

The boy grinned feebly and went out. His heels were loud on the wooden steps going down to the road. Gerard turned and laid bracelets, a jeweled cigarette lighter, and a pack of Players on the coffee table, along with a jeweled watch and an ostrich hide wallet dyed blue. He grunted, getting to his feet. "Not robbery," he said. "All this stuff is real—no costume jewelry here." He picked up the wallet, opened it, drew out money. "Fifty-dollar bills, twenty-dollar bills." He pushed the money back, and let a strip of plastic unfold from the wallet, each pocket with a credit card in it. Gerard wagged his head, folded up the string, glanced at Bohannon. "There was a housebreaker reported in this area today, but he sure as hell didn't stop here."

"Maybe he heard somebody coming before he could get to robbing," Bohannon said. "Mitch getting home from work." He went to look at the rest of the house and came back. Gerard sat at the coffee table, making a list on a sheet of paper with a ballpoint pen. Bohannon said, "He could have run out the back, climbed up through the trees. It's steep, but if a man was scared enough, he could do it."

"We'll look in daylight." Gerard clipped the pen into a shirt pocket, folded the paper, pushed it away. "But I don't think we'll find tracks. Mitch killed her, Hack."

"Ex-cons can't own guns," Bohannon said.

"Must have been Eugenia's." Gerard watched the ambulance crew lay Eugenia on the gurney, cover her with the green blanket, wheel her to the door. The young deputy waited on the deck for them to rattle the wheels over the doorsill, then edged past them and came into the room, holding a revolver upside down, one finger through the trigger-guard. Gerard took it carefully and smiled. "Hey. Thank you, Vern. Good work."

"Mitch didn't take her to sea and drop her overboard," Bohannon said, "He came to me. I don't see that as the act of a guilty man."

"It's how I see flight to avoid prosecution," Gerard said.

"Despair," Bohannon said. He looked around. Fingerprint powder dusted every well-kept surface. He'd seen it in the other rooms, too. He asked Vern, "You do the fingerprint work? Take the photos?"

The lad nodded. "It's all in my car." He read his watch again, and asked Gerard, "We through here now, then?"

Below, the ambulance doors slammed, loud in the night.

"You in a hurry?" Gerard dropped the revolver into his pocket. "Go see all windows and doors are secured, will you? Then you can stand watch outside, okay. Let no one in."

The boy, on his way out of the room, turned back, agony in his face. "My wife's having a baby tonight." He glanced yet again at his watch. "How long do I have to stay?"

"Till the A.M. watch. Everybody's on vacation."

"Well, can I at least sit in the car? T. Hodges said she'd radio me as soon as Tina calls the station."

"You can sit in the car," Gerard said.

Looking miserable, Vern left the room. Bohannon said, "Let him go to the hospital. I'll stand guard here. It's Mitch you expect to show up, isn't it?"

"Wouldn't that be nice?" Gerard said. "You could have your pickup back."

"And you could have your fall guy," Bohannon said. "He won't show up, but maybe somebody will. I haven't anything else to do. I'll stay."

"I'm too short-handed to refuse." Gerard gathered up Eugenia's possessions, stowed them in a pocket. "Thanks."

Below, the ambulance ground its gears and drove off.

"Here's the bullet," Bohannon said, and laid it in Gerard's hand. "Found it in the fireplace, like Belle said. Almost forgot to give it to you."

The noisy county cars, one with Vern in it, headed for the hospital, the other carrying Gerard back to his desk full of work, drove off and quiet settled in. The sea wind whispered in the tall pines. An owl repeated its deep hoot from a high branch. Bohannon walked through the house. In the kitchen, a bottle of Old Grandad stood on the table with a glass that held an inch of melted ice. Cigarette butts filled an ashtray. Bohannon switched off the lights. He did the same in all the other rooms, then leaned in the open doorway to the front deck, and dug cigarettes from his shirt pocket. The pack was mashed, but the contents intact. He lit a cigarette, blew smoke into the darkness, listened, waited. When the cigarette was smoked down, he carried it through to the bathroom and dropped it into the toilet. He flushed the toilet, found aspirin in the medicine chest, washed the tablets down with water from a clear plastic glass. He hoped the aspirin would ease his aches. He switched off the bathroom light, went through the house again to the front deck, and sat on a hard bench there among potted plants. It wouldn't do to get too comfortable. He might fall asleep.

He did fall asleep. Again, he wasn't sure what woke him. But he was alert right away. He got up slowly from the bench, remembered his boots, sat down, and pulled them off. He moved to the stairs and strained to hear. The owl had got his meal and gone silent. But frogs clamored from a faraway pond. The wind still sighed in the trees. He raised his watch close to his eyes, but he couldn't read it. Then a twig snapped on the steps below. His heart thumped. He leaned over the deck rail and squinted down into the dark. He heard labored breathing, a name whispered under the breath. "Genie, Genie." Bohannon backed away from the stairs. A head in a pale hat appeared, a figure in pale clothes, pale shoes that moved without sound.

"Hold it right there," Bohannon said.

And a gun went off. Maybe the pale figure gave a startled cry first. But it only registered with Bohannon later. The gun registered at once. He saw a little burst of fire from the gun and heard the report and felt the wind from the bullet as it passed him, and heard the bullet thump into the wooden wall of the house behind him—all these things at one time. Bohannon hit the deck and rolled. He knocked the shooter's legs from under him. The man went down and the gun went skittering off across the planks of the deck. He didn't see it. He heard it. He pinned the man, face down, to the deck, and bent his arms up behind him. The arms were short, thin, and there was no strength to them. Bohannon sat on the man.

"Who the hell are you, and what do you want here?"

"Ouch," the man said, "you're hurting me."

"You tried to shoot me," Bohannon said.

"You startled me," the man said. "I was frightened."

"On your feet." Bohannon lifted him up. There was nothing to that. He was boy-sized. He kept the arms bent up behind the man and pushed him through the open doorway into the house. He worked the light switch. The man was moon-faced, around forty-five, in a red and blue Hawaiian shirt and green and yellow plaid Bermuda shorts. His straw hat had a dazzling broad ribbon around it. A tourist. All that were missing were the dark glasses and the camera on a strap. Bohannon slowly let him go. "Take it easy, now. Who are you? What are you doing here?"

"I'm a friend of Eugenia Carter," he said, rubbing his arms. "We were in college together."

Bohannon backed out onto the deck, watching the little man, taking only seconds to glance around for the gun. It lay by a redwood planter tub in a corner. He picked it up. "You always bring firearms to call on old friends?"

"I was afraid. It's so dark here. I'm not used to wilderness. Aren't there wild animals?"

"None as wild as you," Bohannon said. "Was she expecting you? Did you phone ahead?"

"No. I wanted to surprise her." The little man took off his hat. He was bald. He wiped his pale dome with a handkerchief and looked around. "Where is she? You're not"—he eyed Bohannon, puzzled—"her husband."

"She's dead. And no, I'm not." The gun was a new .32 revolver. He opened the cylinder. Two bullets were missing. He snapped the cylinder back. "Someone shot her this afternoon." He looked hard into the dazed eyes. "Was it you?"

"Shot her? Dead?" He shook his head violently. "No, oh, no! It wasn't me. No way. This is the first time I was ever here. Right now. Tonight. Oh, God!"

"Then you must have shot a wild animal before, right? What was it? A field mouse?"

"I never shot anything, I swear it. The gun was

151

never full. You're supposed to keep a chamber empty. They told me that when I bought it. It's a safety precaution."

Bohannon sighed. "Show me some identification, please."

He went to the telephone with it and dialed Gerard. "It wasn't Mitch," he said. "It's one Denver Parks from West Los Angeles. You want to come and fetch him proper? Or shall I run him over to you in his car?"

Someone long on dreams and short on common sense had put up a modern building of varnished planks, tinted glass, heavy beams, on a point of land in Madrone at the juncture of two dusty roads. It was a site nobody had been able to make anything of before. The building was all sharp angles and prows. The builder meant to keep a cafe downstairs, rent out the rest of the rooms there for shops, and live in the rooms above. But there was no place but the roads to park on and this meant a climb to reach the place, and the building had stood empty most of the time since. It was good to look at, but not much use. Lately, a young couple had opened the cafe again, but no one else was in it when Bohannon sat by a tall triangular window for lunch with T. Hodges. They were the only customers. They ate chicken wrapped in crepes and covered with a cream sauce, and drank a white wine from a vineyard the other side of the mountains.

"He's just out of a psychiatric hospital," T. Hodges said. "Nervous breakdown following a divorce. He's still shaky, but he's on his way to San Francisco to start life over."

"He should have stayed in his car with his foot on the gas," Bohannon said. "He shouldn't have stopped in Madrone."

"He was taking it easy. Taking in the sights." T. Hodges was dark and trim, with thick eyebrows above lustrous brown eyes that often did her smiling for her—she was self-conscious about her teeth. The upper ones protruded a little. "It's true, he and Eugenia were in the same class at UCLA—twenty some years ago. She says he dated her then."

"Did she carry him in her bookbag?" Bohannon asked.

"That we can't check, can we?" T. Hodges lifted a slim green bottle and poured wine into both glasses. It was a nice brisk wine. The crepes were not so good. Bohannon doubted the cooking here was going to draw crowds. "He was madly in love with her, but after graduation she married a wealthy attorney, old enough to be her father. He died only a few years later—but by that time little Denver Parks was married himself. Still, he never forgot the gorgeous, golden-haired Eugenia. And after he got over the shock of his wife leaving him, he dreamed of finding Eugenia and proposing marriage. Only he didn't really try. It was a fantasy."

"Until he happened to stop for a couple of beers at the Coach & Four yesterday, and there was her picture on the wall, smiling, big as life."

T. Hodges nodded, chewed, swallowed the last of her lunch. "He knew her instantly. He got very excited."

"Mitch would have been on the bar." Bohannon used his napkin, laid it down. "Did he ask Mitch if it was Eugenia?"

"No. Mitch is in that photo, too, remember? He got all shy, afraid maybe Mitch and Eugenia were married."

"So how did he get Eugenia's address?"

"Barbara Duskin came in at six, and Mitch left, and Parks asked Barbara." T. Hodges smiled cautiously, keeping her upper lip over her teeth. "I'll bet you're surprised Barbara Duskin knows her own address, aren't you?"

"I'm not surprised she'd give Eugenia's to a stranger."

A spindly girl of maybe twelve, with straw-color hair and a fiery flush to her cheeks, came to the table to take away the plates. She looked scared of them both, but she swallowed hard, took a deep breath, and said, "Dessert today is apple pan dowdy with clotted cream, or caramel flan, or chocolate mousse torte."

"Coffee, please," Bohannon said, and looked at T. Hodges. "Shall we split an apple pan dowdy between us?" The deputy nodded her sleek, dark head, and Bohannon told the girl child, "One apple pan dowdy, please, and two plates."

"All right," the girl said doubtfully, and went away across the tall, desperately empty room. She didn't balance the plates well, but though they teetered and clanked, they didn't fall. She vanished. In a far, echoing room, they heard her high, thin voice: "They only want one dessert and they're both going to eat it. Is that all right?"

They laughed. Bohannon said, "Mitch left at ten after six. When had Eugenia left, then?"

"No one seems to know. But Parks got there around five, and he says Mitch was alone. And not always present. Parks ran out of cigarettes, needed change for the machine, and had to wait twenty minutes for Mitch to come back to the bar. Mitch said he'd been in the kitchen, making canapés, but Gerard sent somebody to look, and there were no canapés. Did Mitch slip out, drive home, and kill Eugenia?" T. Hodges asked. "And then come back?"

"What for?" Bohannon said.

The spindly youngster came with cups of coffee, frowning, biting her tongue at the corner of her mouth, concentrating on not sloshing coffee into the saucers. She went away.

Bohannon said, "Mitch had time to kill her later, if he wanted to kill her. Parks is lying, isn't he? He killed her, and he's trying to stick Mitch with it."

"When?" she said. "He was in the pub till seven."

"That what Barbara Duskin says?" Bohannon asked.

T. Hodges nodded. "She's terribly upset. Desolated."

"Yup. Who'll give her a job now?" Bohannon drank coffee. "Any other witnesses? Customers?"

"No locals. Only tourists. No way to find them." With quiet, amused eyes, T. Hodges watched the girl solemnly set down a big serving of apple pan dowdy by the vase of marigolds in the center of the table. The dessert steamed under its lathering of cream, and smelled of cinnamon and brown sugar. The girl laid plates in front of them. "Okay?" she said, and when Bohannon reminded her of forks, "Oh, damn." She flounced away in her skinny-ass jeans, running shoes, Madonna T-shirt. T. Hodges said, "You mean he came to Madrone knowing where to find Eugenia and went there before he reached the pub?"

"It's possible."

The girl came and handed them each a fork. The flush was bright in her thin cheeks. "Now—okay?" she asked.

"Okay." Bohannon smiled. "Thank you."

"Thank *you*," she snapped, and this time she ran away.

Bohannon laughed. "Service with a smile."

"Child labor," T. Hodges said grimly. "What are her mom and dad doing back there? Why isn't the child at the beach?"

"You going to issue a citation, officer?" Bohannon asked.

"I'm going to"—she picked up the plate of dessert—"eat my apple pan dowdy." With her fork, she pushed half of it onto Bohannon's plate, the other half onto her own. "Doesn't it smell heavenly?"

"He's still crazy." Bohannon pitched into the concoction, talked with his mouth full. "Why come creeping back in the middle of the night? He'd set Mitch up for the killing. So his reason couldn't have been to steal stuff to make the motive look like robbery. What does he say?"

"That the middle of the night was his only visit." T. Hodges swallowed, drank some coffee. "That he'd been so surprised at finding the girl of his dreams alive and well totally by accident, in a place he'd never been to, never expected to visit, that he was stunned. He drove around and thought about going to see her. But he couldn't work up his nerve. Not till you saw him. It took him hours."

Bohannon said, "How does he explain the gun?"

"Just that he bought it when he knew he was going to travel. He'd never traveled anywhere in his life before. A little tax accountant, working out of his house. Crime was everywhere out there." T. Hodges cringed and rolled her eyes, pantomiming silent-movie fear. "Muggers, drug-crazed killers."

"And wild animals"—Bohannon nodded—"in the dark woods." He worked on finishing off the apple pan dowdy. "Nobody saw him driving around, all those hours, trying to work up his nerve to call on Betty Co-ed?"

T. Hodges peered at him and laughed. "Betty who? What are you talking about?"

"It's an old song," Bohannon said. "You're too young to know about it. Come to think of it, so am I. My mother used to sing it while she did the dishes." He drank some coffee, wiped his mouth, sighed contentment at how good the dessert was, and laid down his napkin. "He give any hint as to why he might have wanted to kill her?"

"He did a little monologue about how she brushed him off with a laugh in college after a few dates," T. Hodges said. "That's not a rational motive. Not after twenty-odd years."

"Maybe she brushed him off with a laugh yesterday." Bohannon pushed back his chair, reached for his wallet. "And who said he was rational? Why didn't that bring back the old hurt again? Obviously he's never forgotten it. Why didn't it drive him over the edge?"

"You ready to go?" she said.

"Yup." Bohannon laid money on the table and rose. "Place might make it, if folks hear about the apple pan dowdy."

"We'll spread the word." She took a last quick gulp of coffee, laid her napkin down, and stood. "Maybe then they can afford to hire a waitress."

Bohannon opened the door for her. A breeze came in. She passed outside beneath his arm. He called back into the handsome, vacant rooms, "Thank you, and good luck," and followed her out onto a varnished deck in bright sunshine. The door fell shut behind them, and they started down the long stairs together, breeze ruffling her hair.

"You're still sure it wasn't Mitch?" she said. "With his record?"

"That's why I'm sure it wasn't Mitch," Bohannon said. "Unless he's crazy, too. And I don't think he is."

He was using the stake truck from the stables until he got his pickup back, if he ever did. The cab of the stake truck smelled of timothy hay, the seat was mended with tape that was peeling off, the floor was tracked with dried manure, and the ride was rough, but T. Hodges didn't seem to mind. They walked together from the parking lot into the substation, where she took the place of an older woman officer at the reception desk, and fastened on a head-set. Bohannon went down the hall to Gerard's office.

Gerard wasn't there, but the file folder with the record of Avery Ames, alias Mitch Russell lay on his desk. Bohannon sat down and read it. When Gerard came in, Bohannon gave him back his chair and asked, "What about the bullet?"

Gerard held out a steaming mug of coffee. "You

want?" Bohannon shook his head, Gerard tried the coffee, set the mug down, and said, "It's from the Russell gun—bought by Eugenia in Beverly Hills, about the time she married Mitch. Ironical, right?"

"That bullet was smashed," Bohannon said.

"The San Francisco police have lab equipment you and I couldn't pay for with our combined lifetime earnings," Gerard said. "They made the match. I believe them."

"What about fingerprints?" Bohannon said.

"Wiped clean," Gerard said.

"So anybody could have used it. Mitch didn't go around with it strapped to his thigh. It was in the house, right?"

"Rules out Parks," Gerard said. "He had his own."

"Maybe," Bohannon said. "Did Belle do the autopsy yet?"

"I stopped by the hospital on my lunch break," Gerard said. "She says death occurred close to five o'clock. There are bruises on her arms. Somebody grabbed them hard."

Bohannon grunted, frowned, sat down. "The time bothers me. The Coach & Four is busy between five and seven. Pass there, you'll hear laughs and clinking ice cubes. Eugenia plays—played—the piano. Golden oldies. Strange time for her to go home. Unless she had an appointment."

"You mean Parks phoned her and set it up?"

"So as not to encounter Mitch. Why not? Parks is crazy. She's his dream-girl. Mitch was at the pub till after six. There was no housebreaker, was there? You didn't find any tracks going up the hill behind the house, did you?"

"Nothing human has climbed that slope in living memory," Gerard said. "But it was a husband-wife thing, Hack. You know it almost always is. A knockdown, drag-out, this time. Mitch was gone from the pub for twenty minutes, remember."

"You've only got Parks's word on that." Bohannon winced and got to his feet. "I wish Mitch hadn't acted so stupid."

"Was it acting?" Gerard said. "I'd say that killing two wives in a row for their money suggests the man was born stupid." He picked up and let fall the file folder on the desk. "Still, he did have a good prison record."

"Model," Bohannon said. "Which sits well with wardens, but not always with the other inmates." He turned for the office door. Gerard's "Meaning?" stopped him. He turned back. "Meaning, I wonder why Mitch had Eugenia buy that gun for him just after he got out of prison. What was he afraid of?"

"You think too much," Gerard said. "Do I hang onto Parks?"

"He tried to shoot me," Bohannon said. "Remember?"

"He thought you were a puma," Gerard said.

"Hang onto him," Bohannon said.

Settlers Cove was being built up fast, but Cholmondeley Road still had most of its pines. The houses stood far apart, a good many of them hidden by the trees, some up above the winding lane, some nestled down below. Roadside mailboxes were all that gave away the presence of most. And parked cars, of course. A few yards down the road and across from the Russell house, a little woman in an electric blue pants suit, a sky blue blouse, and a scarf of many blues, was loading flat, brown-wrapped parcels into the back of an elderly station wagon. Bohannon lurched the stake truck into the shallow ditch, got out, and walked over to her. She was well past sixty, but with a pretty, amused face, and the bluest eyes he had ever seen. She tilted her head at him.

"Something I can do for you?"

He gave her his name and showed her his license. "You see anything unusual over at the Russell place yesterday afternoon? Hear anything?"

"What's happened?" Three more flat parcels leaned on the side of the wagon. With small, freckled hands she laid them one by one on the others in the back of the station wagon. "Something serious, wasn't it? Police cars were there last night. Around ten-thirty. The ambulance. Dr. Hesseltine's car. I went across this morning, but the house is shut up. No one answers at the pub. What's wrong?"

"I was there last night," Bohannon said. "I know about last night. I want to know about the afternoon, around five."

"Is it Eugenia who's sick, or Mitch?"

"She had an accident," Bohannon said. "At five o'clock."

"Oh, no. Poor, lovely thing." The little woman stretched to reach and slam down the door. "She's in the hospital, then?"

"She's dead," Bohannon said. "Someone shot her. And what I want you to tell me is if you heard the shot."

The little woman stared, the blue of her eyes

seemed to fade a little. "Dead? Shot?" She pressed both hands to her mouth and blinked hard to keep tears from coming. "Oh, what a shock!" She looked around at the woodsy place. "Here? A murder? In Settlers Cove? What's the world coming to?" Bohannon looked up with her at the serene blue sky above the swaying tall pines for a moment. He didn't comment. He waited for her. She took a breath, looked at him, and said, "I didn't hear any shot. But I rolled up here to park just after five. I'd been at Stern's gallery in San Luis." Her withered cheeks flushed. "They're giving a show of my paintings." She moved a hand to indicate the parcels in the car. "And I'm helping to hang them."

Bohannon smiled. "I'll have to take a look. What did you see when you got here at five?"

"A young blond girl," the woman said, "come running down the stairs over there. She climbed on a red motor scooter, and she shot off down the road. It wasn't five on the dot. I know. I was ten awful minutes late. Bert gets frantic if I'm not home when I say I'll be. And I'd promised him five."

"Ten after, then," Bohannon said. "You know the girl?"

"Not her name, no. But I've seen her before. She visits the Russells often." The blush came back. "Well—not both of them. She only comes when— Eugenia's out."

"When Mitch is there alone," Bohannon said.

"I hate malicious gossip," she said. "But this is different, isn't it? I'm a witness, aren't I?"

"You sure are," Bohannon said. "Tell me your name."

He parked the stake truck in front of the Coach & Four, beside an old stagecoach with boxes of nasturtiums on its seat and in its windows. The sea breeze had stiffened. It swung the signboard so the hinges creaked. He walked into a patio with flaring bougainvillea in dark shades of red, where there were white metal tables under striped umbrellas. The door to the Coach & Four had diamond-shaped panes of opaque glass and a lock that was no problem to pick. He walked into a small entry hall that had standing racks for hanging coats and hats on. He missed his hat. He'd have to buy a new one. The little entry hall was darkly panelled, and so was the barroom itself. The bar was at the back of the room under racks in which drinking glasses hung upside down. Back of the bar was a long cabinet where a mirror reflected standing bottles of liquor. The bar had elaborate tap handles. At the side of the room, keyboard covered, stood a piano, clean ashtrays stacked up on it, clean glass bowls to hold peanuts, but holding nothing today. The small tables had paper coverings, or plastic, something not cloth. The room smelled of furniture polish and beer. And it was empty and silent.

But he heard a sound in back. He opened the door beside the bar and found himself in a hallway. MEN said a door on one side. LADIES said the one across from it. He moved on and came into a kitchen where a refrigerator hummed. There was no one here. The sound reached him again. He opened a door, but this led into a side room—the room into which the theatre goers came when there were plays. And there were the doors that led into the theatre itself, and it was from beyond those doors that the sounds were coming. Someone was prying nails. He turned the knob of the twin doors, but they were locked. He rapped with his knuckles. No one came.

He let himself out, and walked around back of the building to a dirt parking lot where an old jeep waited under a big, shaggy pepper tree. The back wall of the place was blank white in the sun. He walked to the far side, and here was a set of steps, a stoop, and a door that gaped partway open. He went inside and was backstage of the theatre. The air smelled of greasepaint. The squeal of nails was loud here. It was dark and, used to the brightness outside, he blundered into dusty curtains. He pawed them aside and stepped onto a small stage. A ladder leaned in front of the stage. He saw part of a man standing on the ladder in dirty jeans and worn tennis shoes. Bohannon jumped down off the stage, stood in front of the first row of seats, and looked up at the man.

"What's going on?" Bohannon called.

"I made this." The man was Pete Carmody. "It's mine. I'm taking it home. Mitch says there's not going to be any more theatre. I don't want it boarded up here in the dark. Took me time to make. Why should the termites have it?"

It was a big shield, white, gilt, crimson, with masks of comedy and tragedy, laced with carved ribbons. The inscription read: *All the world's a stage, and all the men and women merely players.* The shield looked heavy. Bohannon wondered how Carmody, skinny and far from young, planned to get it down. "Don't you want help?"

"I am the help." Carmody grunted, prying up

another nail. "I've been the only help Mitch had around here from day one. Oh, I could've acted—did some of that when I was young. But that wasn't what he needed. What he needed was workers. Whoa!" With a groan, the shield came loose and leaned outward. Carmody dropped the crowbar. It bounced at Bohannon's feet. Carmody was leaning forward hard, propping the shield with both hands. The tendons in his scrawny neck stood out, his face turned red. But he went on with his chatter. "Mitch kept asking for volunteers, and getting them. Trouble was when the time came, they didn't show up. Only Pete Carmody, softest touch in town." He began to try to come down the ladder, but when he took a foot off the rung he'd been standing on, to put it on the next rung down, the shield lurched to the side. Carmody grabbed for it frantically, but he couldn't hold it. It crashed to the floor in front of the stage, and split in half. "Damn," Carmody said.

"You should have let me help you," Bohannon said. "We could have rigged a rope and pulley."

"I can put it together with pegs and glue." Carmody came down the ladder. "It'll be okay." He studied Bohannon. "You're the one owns the horse stables up Rodd canyon, right? Used to be a deputy? My name's Carmody."

"Bohannon," Bohannon said, and shook the man's gritty hand. "When was it Mitch told you he was closing the place?"

"Didn't come as a real big surprise," Carmody said. "I could see the way the wind was blowing." He crouched disconsolately by his broken handiwork. "Felt awful about it, though. Place has kept me busy for a year, now. Always loved the theatre.

This was kind of a life's dream come true, you know? I carpentered here, built the sets, painted the flats, rigged up the lights, put in the sound system. I'm going to miss it, damn it. And so are a lot of other retired old coots around here. Made us feel alive. Kept us from going to seed."

"What explanation did Mitch give you?" Bohannon said.

"Didn't have to explain." Sourly, Carmody rose and pushed at the shield with a foot. "I came over yesterday with a copy of the script, to try to work out a light plot. Parked my jeep in back, like always, came in the door back there"—he pointed—"and found Mitch in here, on the stage, bottle of whiskey in his hand, reciting Shakespeare." Carmody turned and waved a thin arm. "To the empty seats. He didn't hear me. I stood and listened. It was Prospero's speech from 'The Tempest.' You know the one—everybody knows it:

> *Our revels now are ended. These our actors*
> *Are melted into air, into thin air;*
> *And like the* (something) *fabric of this vision,*
> *The cloud-capped towers, the gorgeous palaces,*
> *The* (something) *temples, the great globe itself,*
> *Yea, all which it inherit, shall dissolve*
> *And like this insubstantial pageant faded,*
> *Leave not a rack behind: We are such stuff*
> *As dreams are made on, and our little life*
> *Is rounded with a sleep . . .*

I applauded, and he turned around like he'd heard a shot. Damn near dropped the bottle, he was so surprised."

"What time was this?" Bohannon said.

"Quarter past five. I had a lot of fool errands to

run for my wife, took up most of the afternoon. I meant to get here by two. But she kept thinking up this thing and that. Finally dumped the clothes from the cleaners, and ran for my car. She calls, 'Now you be sure and get home for supper,' and I said, 'You'll see me when you see me.' I begged Mitch not to close the theatre. He said it was Eugenia's decision. She held the purse strings. Nothing he could do. It was breaking his heart. There were tears in his eyes. Then he remembered he had customers in the pub, and ran back there."

"He was tending bar alone? Eugenia wasn't there?"

"She went home at five," Carmody said.

"What tipped you off that Mitch was going to close down the theatre? You say you weren't surprised. He told me it was keeping him too busy. Eugenia never got to spend any time with him alone. It was bad for their marriage."

"What was bad for their marriage"—Carmody bent and picked up the crowbar—"was the young girls that came to act in the plays. He couldn't keep his hands off them. Peg McKinley, Sandra Le-Febre, I don't remember all their names. But the last one, Tawny Grimes—her I won't forget."

"Rides a red motor scooter?" Bohannon said. "Blonde?"

"Little sex-pot. Pretty, of course. But that's not hard to be at her age." Carmody snorted. "Seventeen! They know it all, can't tell them anything. I warned her." His mouth twitched. "I won't repeat what she told me to do."

"Warned her of what?" Bohannon said.

"Why, she'd snuggle up to Mitch, nuzzle his ear,

kiss him, put her hand in his pocket—anyplace around here, anyplace at all, any time. 'Eugenia's got eyes and ears,' I told her. 'She's no dummy. None of my business what you and Mitch get up to, but get up to it in private. You'll destroy him, if you keep this up.' " Carmody looked at Bohannon, shook his head, and gave a sour laugh. "Mitch lied to you, Bohannon. It was Tawny Grimes that got this theatre closed down."

The house was weathered wood, maybe five years old, on a street two blocks from the beach in Los Osos. The blacktop on these streets was often covered in sand. The yard of the house was sand. A dimestore wading pool in garish red and yellow stood in the yard, toys floating in it. He stepped around a tricycle on his way past the open garage to the front door. The red motor scooter waited in the garage. Beyond an aluminum screen door, the house door hung open. He heard television sounds,— squeaks, tire-skids, xylophone music. Someone was watching cartoons. He pressed a bell button, and Tawny Grimes came to the door in a little white halter, little white shorts, flip-flap rubber sandals. She squinted at him, reached and clicked the screen door lock, and asked warily, "Who are you? What do you want?"

Bohannon gave his name, showed his license. "You were seen yesterday, running away from the Russell house in Settlers Cove. At five ten in the afternoon. By a neighbor."

"Oh, God," Tawny Grimes said. Then she shook her head. Hard. Blonde hair swirling. "No, it's a lie. I wasn't there. I couldn't be. My mom works part-time. I have to babysit the twins in the afternoons. Every afternoon."

"All you say," Bohannon told her, "the sheriff can check on—you understand that? Eugenia Russell is dead, murdered. Somebody shot her. At just about five o'clock. There was a gun in the house. You were familiar with the house. Flora Weymouth says you visited there pretty often."

"Aren't you the sheriff?" she asked.

"Private investigator," Bohannon said. "But if you'd rather talk to the sheriff, I can get him over here. I just thought maybe you'd prefer to talk to me."

"I didn't kill her," Tawny Grimes said.

"You were having an affair with her husband," Bohannon said. "And Eugenia found out about it, didn't she? So you went to kill her."

"No, no. I didn't." Tears and desperation raised her voice. "I mean—yes, I knew she knew. She telephoned me and said she wanted to talk to me about it, face to face. I was to come to her house at two o'clock, but I said it would have to be five because of the babies. Then my mom was late, so I was late too, right?"

"And she was already dead," Bohannon said.

"How did you know?" Her eyes opened wide.

"I didn't. I only knew you were going to say so. Okay, did you see anybody? Was anybody else in the house?"

"No." She shuddered. "I was too scared. I ran out of there so fast, I almost fell down the stairs."

"What about when you arrived?" Bohannon asked. "Did you see anything or anybody unusual then?"

"What?" She frowned, then her face cleared.

"Yes." She snapped the lock, twisted a squeaky knob, and came outside into the sun. She was excited, and stood close to him, speaking up into his face. "I saw an old wreck of a car, one of those gas-guzzlers, all right? With the paint rubbed off in places, you know, and the chrome all rusty? Upholstery hanging down. It passed me, tearing out of Cholmondeley, just as I got to the crossroads. Almost hit me."

"Did you get a look at the driver?" Bohannon said.

She nodded eagerly. "Dark. With fuzzy hair. He needed a shave. And he had his lips pulled back. Like he was snarling, okay? And his two front teeth were missing."

"Why didn't you call the sheriff?" Bohannon said.

She stepped back. "Are you crazy? And have my folks find out about Mitch and me? They'd ground me for life." The screen door burst open. Two very small humans came out. One male, one female. Both sunburned. Both had little, red swim trunks pulled over their heads. And that was all they had. "Michael," Tawny Grimes said sharply, "Jennifer. Look at you. Get back in that house this minute, do you hear me?" But they only went on giggling, and began chasing each other around and around on the sand.

Bohannon laughed and went away.

"Maybe she made it up," Bohannon said. "But driving over here, I got to wondering about Mitch's time in prison. He's scared to death of going back. He says the inmates are animals. He had Eugenia buy him that gun when he got out."

Gerard was frowning over papers at his desk, shuffling them, making jottings with a ballpoint pen. "Go on."

"Can you check?" Bohannon stood at a window, staring out at the parking lot, watching the moving shadows of the big old trees on the tarmac. "With San Quentin? Maybe some enemy of his in there got out in the last day or two, and came to frame him for murdering his second wife, and send him back to prison. The two missing front teeth ought to help identify him."

Gerard laid down the pen, rocked back in his plastic-cushioned, green metal desk chair. He stretched, yawned. "His name is Hawley Morris Schumacher, Hack. We've got him in a holding cell. He booked into the Sea Breeze motel last night, and this morning he tried to rape the maid when she came to do the room. She knocked him down with a vacuum cleaner, and yelled bloody murder, and when he ran for his car and tried to get it started, a couple of surfers got him."

"You're kidding," Bohannon said.

"He'd been over in Settlers Cove yesterday, all right." Gerard peered into his empty coffee mug. "Walked into three houses—people can't remember to lock up—and took a TV, a VCR, a food processor, a microwave; trunk of his car was full of stuff. I believe Tawny Grimes saw him, all right. But not coming from the Russell place. We tested his hands. He hadn't fired any revolver. And he isn't just out of San Quentin. He's down from Washington state. Skipped parole up there. Where you going?"

"To talk to a nagging housewife," Bohannon said.

When he dropped down out of the stake truck on a worn-out hook of road behind Madrone, he looked for the old jeep anyplace around the plain white one-story house, and didn't see it. The roof of the house sagged, and its silver-green composition shingles needed to be replaced. He climbed a pot-holed driveway of pebbly gray blacktop and saw out back a shacky garage. The doors stood open. Inside was a workshop, all kinds of saws and drills and planers. Tools hung over a workbench. Coils of wire hung from rafters. Lengths of one by twos, two by fours, four by fours lay along the rafters. So did lengths of lead pipe, copper tubing. There were metal racks of small drawers for nails and screws and the like. No rolls of roofing paper. Bohannon laughed to himself and went along the side of the house to the kitchen door. Front doors in neighborhoods like this got little use. He rapped an old wooden screen door.

The woman who called, "Who's that?" in a fluty voice, and then appeared at the door, wiping her hands on an apron, didn't look like a nag. She was plump and rosy. A strand of gray hair fell over a forehead damp from cooking heat. Her eyes were brown and shiny. "Oh." She looked startled. "I don't know you." She looked doubtful. "You're not selling something? We're retired people. We have no money."

"I'm not selling anything." Bohannon explained who he was, showed his license yet again. "There's been a death," he said. "Eugenia Russell."

"Oh, dear." She reached and unhooked the screen door, and pushed it open so he could come in. "That's sad. She was a young woman. It's about the theatre, then. You'll be wanting to talk to my husband."

"No, I've talked to him," Bohannon said. "I don't see his car here. So let me ask you. There's something I think I didn't get straight. He told me he'd run a lot of errands for you, yesterday afternoon."

She'd gone to a counter, a butcher-block bread-board, and was kneading dough, watching him as she punched it down, turned it over, folded it, punched it down again. Now she stopped and frowned, pulling away dough that had stuck to her fingers. "He did? I wonder why? We get mixed up sometimes, as we get older. I hope you don't, but I expect you'll learn that in time."

Bohannon smiled. "I expect so. You didn't send him out again and again? To the dry cleaners, for example?"

"Oh, dear, no. The dry cleaners was on Monday." She laughed sadly to herself, and wagged her head. "Yesterday, as a matter of fact, he went out about a quarter to two, I'd say. Said it was about the theatre. He spends a lot of time puttering around down there, you know. He complains about how hard Mitch works him, takes him for granted, all that nonsense, but he really loves it. He'd be lost without it." She quit kneading again, laughed, pushed the strand of hair back with the back of a wrist. "And I'll be honest—it's nice having him out from underfoot sometimes."

"What time did he come home yesterday?" Bohannon said.

"Five-thirty," she said. "He seemed very happy."

"He didn't say why?" Bohannon asked.

"Oh, he'd been afraid the theatre was going to close." She rattled pans out of a lower cupboard, set them side by side on the counter. "I don't know what it was all about." She dipped fingers into a can of shortening and went to greasing the pans. "I listen to him talk about the theatre, of course. I say, 'Mn-hmm,' and 'is that so?' and 'well, that sounds wonderful,' but I really don't hear. It's never been interesting to me. I'm just happy for Pete."

"I understand," Bohannon said.

She plopped white loaves of dough into the pans. "And yesterday, he had good news. The theatre wasn't going to close after all." She bent and opened the oven door of an old range. The spring twanged. She set the pans inside, and closed the door. She turned and faced him, wiping her hands on her apron again. "There. That's done. Oh, listen. I haven't been hospitable at all. It's a warm day. How about some iced tea?"

"No, thanks," Bohannon said. "But can I use your phone?"

Gerard said, "He went out at a quarter to two because he'd overheard Eugenia on the telephone at the Coach & Four tell Tawny Grimes to meet her at home at two. He figured she'd be there alone and he could plead with her not to make Mitch close the theatre. She wasn't there, of course. He hadn't heard all the conversation, hadn't heard Tawny

Grimes, at the other end of the line, change the time to five, because of her baby-sitting obligations."

It was near sundown. Bohannon stood with whiskey and ice in a plastic glass and gazed out the window again. He smoked a cigarette. Across the highway, the pines of Settlers Cove were silhouetted against a sky that kept changing colors—from blue to green, from green to gold, from gold to fiery red. Gerard sat at his desk, knot of his tie pulled down, collar open, beard stubble showing. It had been a long day. The whiskey had come from a bottle in the bottom drawer of his desk. He opened the drawer again, now, and tilted the bottle a second time over his own plastic glass. He held the bottle out to Bohannon, who shook his head, and when Gerard had capped the bottle, put it back into the drawer, shut the drawer, said:

"So he waited, did he? All that time?"

"No." Gerard worked on his whiskey. "He figured he'd miscued, and he drove the jeep back to the theatre and hung around, fiddling with this and that, till he heard Eugenia's car start up out back. Then he followed her home."

Bohannon stepped to the desk to flick ashes from his cigarette into a green metal wastebasket. "And that was a little before five, right? And he begged and pleaded and argued with her, and when he wouldn't take no for an answer, and refused to leave, she got the gun."

Gerard nodded wearily. "From a sideboard in the dining area. And he wasn't having that, not from a woman. He stepped up to take the gun away from her, and she put up a struggle. That's when her heel broke, like as not. And then, somehow, he had the gun in his hand, and was backing away, when it went off. That's how he tells it. It just fired, all by itself. He didn't mean to kill her."

"She's just as dead as if he did," Bohannon said.

Gerard gave his head a grim shake, and drank more whiskey. "I don't know why people won't phone us, why they think they have to settle these things themselves. With guns. She seemed brighter to me than that."

Bohannon grunted, bent over the wastebasket, snubbed out his cigarette on the metal. His bruises ached and he straightened up, wincing. "He was happy when he got home—did I tell you? Told his wife the theatre wasn't going to close, after all. What do you think—is he senile?"

"He was sly with you," Gerard said, and drank some more whiskey. "Taking his work of art out of there today, telling you it was going to close, mourning about it. Giving no inkling he knew Eugenia was dead. Trying to frame Tawny Grimes for the murder. Not senile. I don't think so."

"He knew when Eugenia had left the Coach & Four." Bohannon finished off his whiskey, dropped the empty glass into the wastebasket with a rattle. "No one else did, barring Mitch, of course." Bohannon walked heavily toward the office door. "That bothered me, when I came to think about it."

"I take back what I said," Gerard said.

Bohannon's hand was on the doorknob. "What was that?"

"That you think too much." Gerard rose and gave him a tired smile. "You've done it all, Hack. And I appreciate it. You're one smart cop. You ought to come back to work."

"You know better than that," Bohannon said, and left.

Bohannon limped in at the kitchen door. "Sorry I'm late." Plates lay on the table, glinting in the last glow of sunset through the windows. A big bottle of ketchup glinted too. It was a fixture in the middle of the table whenever Stubbs cooked. The air of the big plank room was rich with good smells. Bohannon dragged out his chair, sat at his place. Stubbs, a fat, ruddy old man, turned from the stove, came holding with quilted oven mittens a brown crockery pot. He set it on a pad and lifted the cover. "See," he said, "you ruined my soufflé."

"Looks like beef and beans to me," Bohannon said.

"Started out a soufflé," Stubbs said. "You being late turned it like that."

"What's this?" Bohannon picked up the newspaper that lay folded beside his plate, while Stubbs used a big spoon to ladle onto that plate plump beans in a rich sauce of molasses laced with mustard. Chunks of browned and tender beef came with the beans. The headline on the paper Stubbs had turned up for him to see read POPULAR BAR OWNER SLAIN, HUSBAND SOUGHT. Bohannon laid the paper down. "Not any more," he said, and tucked a napkin in at the collar of his shirt. "It was Pete Carmody who killed her."

Stubbs, wrapped in an apron, dishing out his own supper from the pot, blinked at him. "The skinny old guy? The handyman?" Stubbs left the spoon sticking out of the pot, set the cover on, pulled off the mittens, untied his apron and laid it with the mittens on an empty chair. "What in the world for?" He sat down to eat, smacking his lips.

And Bohannon told him what for.

"Well, in that case"—Stubbs had been ruining his beans with a big dousing of ketchup, and now set down the ketchup bottle, and pushed back his chair—"I can let my prisoner go."

Bohannon stared at him in the shadows. "What are you talking about?"

"Ruby wandered off this morning." Stubbs got painfully to his feet. He had been a rodeo rider the first half of his life and it had left him pretty well crippled up in the second half. "And you know where she always goes when she takes these fits. Up the box canyon. So I rode up there with a bridle to lead her back."

Bohannon looked around the dim table. "Bread?"

"Doggone it," Stubbs said, and hobbled off to get a loaf, a knife, and from the refrigerator a cold chunk of butter. "I'm recounting a fascinating anecdote here. Can't you forget your stomach for a minute?"

"Have to have bread"—Bohannon sawed a slab from the loaf—"to mop up the gravy. You know that. And it's not fascinating." He wiped the bread around the beans and beef on his plate. "Ruby pulls that stunt all the time."

"Ruby's only the prologue," Stubbs said. "I'd started back with her, when I seen the crossbar on the doors of the shed up there is missing. Lock's busted. I got down to have a look inside. And guess what's in there? Your pickup."

"You're kidding," Bohannon said.

"And guess who's sitting in it, sound asleep?"

"Mitch Russell," Bohannon said. "How about that?"

"So I backed out real quiet, shut the doors, and put the crossbar back. And I guess it's time to go let him out, isn't it?"

"I hope he's got my hat," Bohannon said.

Death of an Otter

The bunch of flowers in his hand caught her attention for a moment, no more than that. She turned her head away. He had got used to how short they kept her hair. It made her head look like a small boy's, and the absence of makeup added to that effect. Never mind. Her head was a beautiful shape, and her skin and features were good—she'd never needed makeup. This visit was the same as always. When the nurse opened the door to her room, and he saw her seated in sunlight from a window, and the nurse said cheerfully, "Look who's come to see you," and she turned that brief, blank look on him, his heart made as if to surge out of his chest.

He wanted to rush in and take her in his arms, and hold her close, as he had done a thousand times in their lost years together. But he couldn't do that. Once long ago, when the doctor had told him she seemed better, less withdrawn, more her old self, Hack had tried it. It was a mistake he'd never forget. She had watched him come to her without a sign of alarm, but when he'd put his hands on her shoulders, she'd started to scream. Her eyes filled with horror. She beat and scratched at him, kicked at him, writhed, struggled. Nurses, attendants, a doctor had come. She was sedated in a few short minutes. But to him, her screaming seemed to go on and on.

It wasn't him she was frightened of. He knew that. She was back again in those nightmare hours aboard a stinking tub of a fishing boat up from Mexico with a cargo of brown heroin. That night was long ago, but it looked as if she was going to live in it forever. The early hopes of the doctors had proved wishful thinking. Her times of drugged calm grew longer, but she never once spoke. And when the terror swept over her, it was as if no time at all had passed. He blamed himself for letting the *metedors* take her, though he didn't fairly see how he could have prevented it, even if he'd forseen it. It had happened fast.

Hardest of all to live with was that somehow he ought to have forseen it. He had been a peace officer for a dozen years when it happened. He had them, and they knew he had them—unless they crippled him. And they did that by snatching Linda. Then he'd lost his head, and called for back-up. His fellow officers had dropped the *metedors* bloody and dead in the bottom of their boat. They'd given Hack Bohannon back his wife. But they'd been too long getting there, and she was lost to him. He sat now in a creaky white wicker chair opposite her, and talked quietly about his stables, his horses, the horses he boarded for others.

She looked at him sometimes, briefly. He wasn't sure what understanding, if any, was in those looks. But once, when he was telling her about this spring's foals, wobbling up from the straw on their spindly legs, he thought she smiled for a second. Maybe not. Maybe it was the shadow of leaves from the tree outside the window touching her mouth.

But he wanted to believe it was a smile. When the nurse came with a vase for the flowers and by glancing at her watch indicated it was time for him to leave, and he rose with his sweat-stained Stetson in his hand—he wanted to bend and kiss the mouth where that possible smile had appeared. But he only said, "Be good. I'll be back next Monday." Out in the cool, dim hallway of the lumbering old house, he wondered why he'd said such a damned fool thing. She'd never been any way but good in her life.

Gloom always settled in him after these visits. He had never brought anyone along before. Today he had brought T. Hodges, a young deputy from the sheriff station where he used to work. She was the first woman friend he'd made since he and Linda had been wrenched apart. She was very different. Oh, slight like Linda, yes, but dark, with a way of smiling with her eyes because she was self-conscious about her teeth—the upper ones stuck out a little. He wasn't sure why she'd asked to come along with him today. Maybe because she sensed the visits were hard for him and made him feel more than commonly alone.

He judged her to be too young to have to face this kind of situation, even at secondhand. He'd told her no before. Then, because it seemed to hurt her, this time he had said yes. But she'd been troubled on the ride over the mountains from the coast, and quiet. She'd got out of the old pickup and walked with him across lawns past flowerbeds in the morning sunshine. Quiet. She'd even climbed the steps to the great verandah of the house, but there she had lost her nerve. He'd crossed the porch to the door and rung the bell before he missed her and looked back. She stood at the top of the steps, tears glistening in her dark eyes, and shaking her head. "I can't," she said. "I'll wait here."

He came out onto the porch now, put on his Stetson, looked for her. She was far off across a downhill sweep of grass, sitting alone on a green bench under a willow. He went down the steps slowly, and stood at the foot of the steps and waited for her to come to him. She came, at a slow walk, head hanging. When she reached him, she looked up, ashamed. "I guess I'm a coward," she said. "I didn't know that. I'm sorry, Hack. I wasn't any help to you at all, was I?" He gave her a small hug, left the arm over her shoulder, started with her toward the truck. "How was she?" T. Hodges asked.

"She almost smiled today," he said. He twisted the rusty handle, pulled open the rusty-hinged cab door for her. She climbed up and sat on the cracked, tape-mended seat. He slammed the door, went around and got in at the driver's side, slammed that door, the tinny sound loud in the mountain stillness. The cab smelled of timothy hay and of the dried manure underfoot on the tattered rubber floor mat. He keyed the engine noisily to life. "Ah, hell," he said. "I'm making it up. She was just the same today. She isn't getting any better." He let the handbrake go, and rolled the rattly truck off across crackling gravel.

Along highway one north of Madrone, buildings had gone up lately—motels, and places to eat. Stucco and neon. He didn't like them. When there'd come a chance, he'd voted against them. He'd written a protest letter to the local weekly paper. He'd never run into anyone who wanted them. Yet up they went, didn't they? Here, damn it, was a whole new shopping center—boutiques, boulangeries, cafés serving nothing but crepes. Then there were isolated hamburger joints and fried shrimp counters. A good many hadn't made it. Some stood boarded up, bleak in the cold spring sunlight off the ocean. Others kept changing hands.

Here was an ugly white place repainted, paper banners taped to it, GRAND OPENING, last Saturday's date. A woman in a green down jacket and blue jeans was up on an aluminum ladder yanking the highest of these signs down. She turned her head so he saw her face just as he passed. He was startled, and put a foot on the brake pedal. He edged off onto the road shoulder. T. Hodges looked at him curiously. "Somebody I used to know," he said, and watched the dusty side mirror until the highway was clear, and swung onto it, and headed back for the place. She was tearing down the paper signs from the windows now. He got down from the truck and walked over to her. "Dorothy Hawes?" he said.

She turned, the wadded paper signs clutched in her arms. The sea wind blew her gray hair across her eyes. But she saw who he was. And showed alarm before she caught herself and smiled. "Why, Hack Bohannon. How are you?"

"When did you come back?" he said.

"A few weeks ago," she said, and tossed her head to let the wind blow the hair off her face. "I should have let you know, but I've been busy setting up shop here."

"How long has it been?" he said. "Twenty years?"

"Eighteen," she said, "but I never thought of it as anything but temporary. I hated Los Angeles." She gave a shudder that had nothing to do with the wind chill factor. "But work was easier to find there. I was on my own, wasn't I?" Her young husband had drowned, leaving her with two girls scarcely more than babies. "Mouths to feed, and all that. Sometimes we need cities, no way around it."

T. Hodges walked up, interested. Bohannon said, "Dorothy Hawes, Teresa Hodges. She's a deputy sheriff."

"And you? You must be a captain by now." Dorothy Hawes's blue eyes rested for a moment thoughtfully on him. "You were the best they had. The one who cared."

Bohannon shook his head. "I quit some time back. I keep horses now. Up Rodd canyon."

The Hawes woman said, "I'm not surprised. There's no justice in this world." She turned away. "Come on. Have lunch. I'm in need of customers." She laughed, struggling, arms filled with the crumpled paper, to open the door. He opened it for her. They all went inside. The restaurant, white and cold as the innards of a refrigerator, smelled good. The smells came warm from the kitchen, onions and herbs, chilis, cheeses. "You've got your choice of tables." Hawes made for the kitchen swing door, calling out something in Spanish to whoever was beyond it. She vanished, but she was back in a minute, unburdened of the signs.

"We planned to picnic on the beach," T. Hodges said.

"All right. I think I can scare up a picnic basket. How does chicken sound? Rotisseried. Mustard and honey glaze? You'll love it. A slab of Monterey jack? Sourdough bread delivered by hand fresh from San Francisco this morning? My wine license isn't here yet, but I'll slip you a bottle of something wonderful, if you promise not to tell." She grinned at T. Hodges. "Or am I suborning you?"

"Not if you let me pay for it."

"It will only take two minutes." Dorothy Hawes bustled back to the kitchen. "And you'll be on your way."

The basket stood on rough rocks. The wind off the ocean was strong. A tablecloth had been folded into the basket, but they didn't try to lay it out, nor to set plates and glasses on it. They tore the chicken apart with their hands, ate with their fingers. Bohannon used his clasp knife to cut the bread and cheese. The wine was good, bright and clean-tasting. Everything was delicious. The sea air helped make it that way. But the wind was too cold to invite sitting still for long. They closed up the bones and crusts in the basket, climbed down to the sand, and walked.

It hadn't been a talky lunch, and they didn't talk as they walked, either. The only sound was the slap and slither of the surf on the sand, and the crunch of their soles in the sand. The water, moiling around shoreward rocks, was a dozen different shades of blue and green. Out farther, beds of brown kelp rose and fell heavily on the sparkling swells. Bohannon felt good that T. Hodges was with him. The gloom was lifting already.

Then they rounded a clump of rocks. She was a couple of steps ahead of him, she gasped, she stopped in her tracks. And he saw what she saw. Lying in the surf, thick fur matted, eyes half shut and glazed over, stiffened body rolling in the wash of the tide was a sea otter, a big fellow, maybe sixty pounds. A dark hole was in the skull behind the left ear. Hack knew it for a bullet hole before he passed the basket to T. Hodges, crouched, and picked the dead animal up. Cradling it, heavy, cold, wet against him, he started back along the beach to find the truck. T. Hodges had recognized the bullet hole, too. She hurried after him.

"I can't believe it," she panted. "He was drunk. Nobody thought he meant it."

"Looks like he did," Bohannon said.

Madrone had a white barn of a building for meetings. In the big pine plank hall dances were held, rummage sales when rain and cold and wind sent folks indoors, community suppers, shows of paintings by local artists, political gatherings in election years. Last night, the folding chairs that often stood in stacks along the walls, were brought out into the middle of the room and set up in rows. Some were metal, some wood, but none was empty by the time the meeting got underway. The dirt parking area outside was jammed with cars. Cars stood along the road shoulders, too, north and south.

The meeting was about sea otters. The inshore waters off Madrone, and for about two hundred miles up and down the coast from Monterey to Morro Bay were a sea otter refuge. Once nearly wiped out by fur hunters, the animals had come back under government protection. There were nearly two thousand now, breeding, feeding, playing in the massive kelp beds. Tourists parked alongside highway one to watch them through binoculars. They were clownish eaters, lying on their backs, flat rocks on their chests, cracking abalone, sea urchins, spiny lobsters against the rocks, stuffing their mouths. Gulls circled for scraps. It made a show.

But it didn't amuse the men who once made a living here diving for abalone. An adult sea otter can eat twelve pounds of abalone in a day. It didn't amuse the operators of fishing boats who had been forbidden to use gill nets in the shallow waters to catch halibut. Too many otters got caught and drowned in gill nets. Now the federal government, worried about offshore oil rigs coming into the area, proposed moving some of the sea otters to an island off southern California, in case there were oil spills. So there would be a seed colony, in case the central coast otters all died.

A good many speakers took the microphones at the meeting. An oil company spokesman, in a shirt and tie, said there was no risk to the otters. Sturdy old Sharon Webb, in jeans and hiking boots, who'd spent decades battling to save nature from the ravening greed of men, said the translocation was well worth a million tax dollars. A commercial fisherman from down the coast who made his living off the abalone around the island protested. Everyone got his or her say. Bohannon found the slat seat of the wooden folding chair hard under his butt after awhile, and kept looking at his watch. The meeting went on a long time, mostly in circles. But fireworks broke out at the end, and all who stayed got some excitement to cut the boredom and send them home with something to talk about before bedtime.

Brick Lightner had a seat down toward the front, where the federal and state wildlife people sat at a table facing the crowd, trying to field questions, and monitor speeches. Lightner, a balding, bony man in a torn, greasy leather jacket, had called out more than once, "Aw, sit down and shut up," during this talk and that. Afterwards, someone said he'd kept mumbling "Goddam commies" under his breath. And firing up his breath from a pint whiskey bottle in his jacket pocket. But he'd made no effort to get a microphone and talk himself.

Until the chairman, a young naturalist for the Wildlife Service, a sunburned kid who kept an eye on the otters through a telescope from Piedras Blancas lighthouse during business hours, said it was late, and made polite remarks about how important it had been to hear all sides of the question, and how other local meetings like this would be held up and down the coast before any decision was made, and thanked everybody for coming.

Then Lightner roared to his feet, shouting, waving his angular arms, his long, stringy, reddish hair flying. "We don't need no more meetings. Jesus Christ, isn't there one suffering soul in this room with a little common sense? Just what did a damn sea otter ever do for you? Any of you. Can you answer that? Did a sea otter ever give you a dollar for a loaf of bread or a gallon of gas? Did a sea otter ever pay your rent or the taxes to send your kids to school?"

People had already started scraping up out of their chairs to leave, but nobody left. Not now. Some stood in front of their chairs, many with arms half into coats they had begun to put on. Some sat down again. But nobody said anything. Everybody listened, a good many of them with mouths half opened—making themselves look to the viewer as stupid as Lightner seemed to think they were, though Bohannon knew they weren't. Lightner raved on:

"You know the answer to that. The answer is 'no.' But I'll tell you who does give you a dollar now and then, who does pay your rent and taxes. Me, and men like me. And where do we get those dollars? From abalone and halibut, that's where. My old man fished this coastline thirty years and me after him. Until the goddam government let those useless animals in here to eat up everything under water and leave nothing for us. Nothing."

He had been facing the crowd. Now he turned and jabbed a knuckly finger at the government people at the table. "And now you come telling us you're going to take two hundred fifty of these devouring locusts and put them someplace else on the coast to take away the honest livelihood of other fishermen. Because the sea otter is an 'endangered species' "—he spoke the words with a mincing sneer—"and has to be protected." Spittle had collected on his mouth. He wiped at it angrily with the back of a hand.

"Well, let me tell you who's the endangered species. It's you and me. Hell, there's two hundred thousand sea otters up off Alaska. Maybe more.

Too many to count. To listen to folks talk here to-night, you'd think if we don't watch out, sea otters was going to disappear any minute now off the face of the deep. Well, they ain't. But I'll tell you where they are gonna disappear from. They're gonna dis-appear from this stretch of coast right out here." He made a wide gesture with a ragged arm. "And do you know how? It won't be the government that does it. For a million dollars. It'll be you and me, my friends, my fellow citizens." He managed a kind of crazy smile, now, and a crazy-wise nod of his head. "We are gonna vote.

"And I'll tell you how we're gonna vote. Ain't a pickup truck around here hasn't got a rifle racked up over the back window. Now, you know that's so. I don't quite know why. Hasn't been a bear sighted around here in twenty years. Hasn't been a cougar. They don't let you shoot the deer. Those rifles are there because it's your God-given right as an Amer-ican to have them there, and that's enough. It's in the Constitution."

"Go home, Brick," somebody shouted. "Sleep it off."

"Wait a minute. I said we was gonna vote. And I'll tell you how. We're gonna vote with bullets. Gonna put them rifles to some use. Every man jack here is going down to the beach tomorrow at sunup, take that rifle down, and shoot himself half a dozen sea otters."

People jeered, moaned, and began to leave.

"Hold on. You want to solve this problem or not? All these sons of"—he waved drunkenly at the ta-ble—"bureaucrats are gonna do is talk, talk, talk. We have to eat, we have to feed our kids. Sea otters are nothing but vermin. Getting a few of them out of here won't change nothing. Still won't be no abalone. Still can't drop gill nets. They all gotta go. And I promise you, I'll kill my share. And if the rest of you got any guts, you'll be out there with me tomorrow, and do likewise. If we don't do it, nobody will. Use your common sense."

But by this time, no one was listening anymore.

When they swung in at the sheriff's station and parked on the leached asphalt of the lot there, under the high hedge of big, old, ragged eucalyptus trees, it was time for T. Hodges to go to work. They got out of the truck. The truck bed was strewn with grit, straw, spilled oats. Bohannon lifted the stiff carcass of the otter out of it, and followed T. Hodges into the station through the side door. He stopped at Gerard's office. She gave him a small smile, and went on out to the reception and communications desk in the front room.

Bohannon worked the knob of Gerard's door awkwardly, pushed the door with his shoulder, stepped in, and laid the damp dead body of the otter on the floor. Gerard was seated back of his desk, talking on the telephone. He watched Bohannon with raised brows, told the caller, "I'll get back to you," and set the receiver in place. He stood up and came around the desk, and stood staring down at what Bohannon had brought him. Sea water pooled around the dark form on the sleek vinyl tiles. "Son of a bitch," Gerard said. "He went and did it."

"I don't know if there are any more," Bohannon said. "I didn't look. I just came with this one."

"There better not be any more," Gerard said darkly. "What a crazy fool." He dropped disgusted into his chair again. "I knew the day his mother died, we were in for it. Nance was the only one who could control him."

Bohannon grunted. "Some of the time."

"Well, she broke his bottles," Gerard said. "That helped. I'm only saying, this is the worst."

"The fine is twenty thousand dollars, which I don't think he's got. He'll lose his boat. Maybe his house."

"He won't need them," Gerard said. "He'll be in jail for a year. Maybe the worst was that last time he beat up Lucille. Blood all over the kitchen. Little Nolan screaming in a corner. When I saw her face, I thought she was a goner. She didn't look human anymore."

"I wasn't here for that," Bohannon said.

"No, I'm wrong again," Gerard said. "The worst was Bob Hawes drowning."

"The storm did that," Bohannon said. "Wonder was, everybody on board didn't drown. Yes, Brick was the skipper, and he shouldn't have been drunk. But Bob's death wasn't his fault. The jury was right."

"I guess so." Gerard looked at the open door of the office and shouted, "Vern!" An echoing "Hoy!" came from someplace in the building. Heels thumped the hallway. A fair-haired young fellow in uniform appeared in the doorway. Gerard told him, "Take Tommy with you, and go pick up Brick Lightner. You know where he lives? Charge him with—"

"Aw, no." Vern saw the otter on the floor. He looked stricken. He stepped into the office and crouched over the dead animal. "Shot?" His voice wobbled. He stroked the brown fur. "Aw, hell." He looked up at Gerard, tears in his eyes. "This? You mean that crazy drunk did this?"

"He threatened it last night," Bohannon said. "Everybody at the meeting heard him."

Vern pushed grimly to his feet. "Okay, we'll pick him up." He started out of the room, swearing under his breath.

"Vern," Gerard cautioned. "Keep your temper."

"Yessir," Vern said. In the hallway, he called out, "Tommy, let's go." And two pair of boots banged off toward the parking lot door. It slammed behind the young officers. Gerard lifted the telephone receiver and said to Bohannon:

"I'll notify Fish and Wildlife. You want to get us some coffee?" His finger hesitated over the push buttons. "Where did this happen?"

On his way out, Bohannon turned back. "Old Bull Cove. You know it? The kid in the lighthouse couldn't have seen it. There's a tall bluff."

"I know it." Gerard nodded and punched the buttons. Bohannon went for the coffee. It simmered in a glass urn on a hot plate near T. Hodges's desk. She was wearing her headphones and little mike on its curved wand, and her hands were busy on a keyboard typing up records. He carried mugs of coffee back to Gerard's office. The lieutenant was on his knees, examining the otter. "Looks like a thirty-thirty. That's what Lightner owns." He got to his feet and accepted the mug, steam curling on the surface of the coffee. "Sit down," he told Bohannon, and went around back of the desk again, and sat down there.

Bohannon stepped over the otter and took a chair. "Wildlife going to patrol the beach, looking for more?"

"Right," Gerard said. "They'll pick this one up and give it a thorough going over. They sounded grim."

"I don't remember it ever happening before." Bohannon poked into the ragged breast pocket of his old Levi jacket for a cigarette, lit the cigarette, pawed in the papers on Gerard's desk for an ashtray, dropped the kitchen match into it. "There's a stiff fine for even taking firearms onto the beach. Signs posted all along the highway."

"Yeah, well—" The phone rang, and Gerard picked it up. He listened for a few seconds, grimaced, said, "Okay, forget him for now. Go talk to Lucille Dodson. See why she didn't report it." He banged the receiver down. "Lightner's not home. His boat's out. At the dock, they say he took it out at dawn."

"Carrying his gun?" Bohannon said.

"In plain sight." Gerard nodded. "But there's worse news than that. He had little Nolan with him."

The Dodson place stood among pines in Settlers Cove, a handsome place of redwood planks, decks, glass, strong, angular beams. Eliot Dodson was some kind of electronics whiz, a troubleshooter whose work took him off on jets a good many times in a year. Sometimes as far away as India and Japan. After that last awful beating Brick had given Lucille, she'd been in the hospital a long time, while they put her broken face back together. She had met Dodson there when he was recovering from intestinal surgery of some sort. They had married when Lucille's divorce from Lightner was final. Lucille had won custody of the one child, a freckle-faced, red-haired boy of seven named Nolan after a famous baseball pitcher.

The tan and gold county car with the strip of lights along its top stood at the foot of zig zag wooden steps that led up to the Dodson house. The radio inside the car crackled on and off. Bohannon braked his pickup on the winding road to let Gerard out. Gerard worked the door, opened it, jumped down, turned. "Can't you spare the time? I'd like you to hear what she says."

Bohannon looked at his watch, grimaced, reached across and closed the passenger door, then wheeled the truck to the road edge and left it angled in the ditch. Between them, old George Stubbs and young Manuel Rivera would keep everything going at the stables till he turned up—though he didn't feel it was fair to leave them to it for so long. He followed Gerard up the stairs. The two young officers were standing in a big room with a field-stone fireplace, talking to Lucille, who was also standing. She was fair-haired and slender. Married to Brick Lightner, she'd dragged around in jeans and sweaters, hands chapped, hair ragged, looking twice her age. Marriage to a decent man had changed that. She stood straight now, and though anybody with half an eye could see her face had been patched up, she looked prettier than she ever had at Brick's.

"Mrs. Dodson?" The glass sliding door to the front deck, that was strewn with the long brown needles from the pines that crowded around, stood open and Gerard stepped through it. "Lieutenant

Gerard." He nodded his head back to indicate Bohannon, and spoke Bohannon's name by way of introduction. Lucille gave them a mechanical smile.

Vern said to Gerard, "Brick walked in and took Nolan out of his bed and the boy was dressing when Mrs. Dodson heard them talking, and went in to see."

"It was four-thirty in the morning," she said. "He had no right to come here, you know. There's a court order. He can't come within two hundred yards of this place."

"She told him not to take the boy," Vern said.

"He'd lost the right even to see Nolan," she said. "For touching him, he could go straight to prison."

"But he had a gun," Bohannon said.

She nodded bitterly. "And I think he would have used it. He was terribly drunk. He could be that way and still walk around. A crazy look in his eyes. It was this sea otter business. He was going to kill them all. From his boat. And no one would be able to punish him for it—not if he had Nolan with him. If they tried to capture him"—her voice trembled, and she bit her lower lip hard so as not to start to cry—"he'd kill Nolan and himself."

"And you believe that?" Gerard said.

She eyed him coldly. "Would you take a chance, if it was your little boy?"

"No, ma'am," Gerard said. "I guess I wouldn't."

"He said not to set the law after him," Vern said.

Gerard looked at her. "And you didn't." He held up a hand. "No, wait. You didn't notify us. We came to you because someone at the dock saw Brick with the boy when he took his boat out this morning. You didn't do anything he told you not to. Remember that. Rest easy with that."

"Are you going to call the Coast Guard?" she said. "For the death of one animal, you're going to force him to murder his own son?"

"We won't let that happen," Gerard said. "But I wish you'd reported this as soon as he left here. We might have stopped him before he got to the boat."

"I was afraid for Nolan. No"—she shook her head angrily—"what I should have done was follow them in my car and make him take me along. My mind wasn't working."

"It happens to all of us." Bohannon remembered again the time with the smugglers. "Where's your husband?"

"Seattle," she said numbly. "He's flying to San Francisco. He'll drive down from there."

"That's good." Gerard turned for the door, turned back again. "Try not to worry. Brick's got a loud mouth, you know that. But it's one thing to beat up your wife, it's another to go up against a whole community."

"He killed that otter, Lieutenant. He isn't thinking like a normal person. He says he has nothing more to lose."

"He won't kill his son," Bohannon said. "As for himself—we're all scared of dying, when it comes down to it. He'll turn up with his tail between his legs. You'll see."

She regarded him steadily for a moment, wondering, worrying. Then she drew breath, said, "Thank you," to them all, and they trooped out, heavy-footed, boots noisy on the deck planks and the steps going down. Someplace distant, a blue jay squawked in the afternoon silence of the pines.

Horses waken with the sun. And Hack had worked a couple of hours in the stables when he came into the pine plank kitchen at seven forty-five. The place was aromatic with breakfast smells. Stubbs, wrapped in a mighty apron, worked at the towering old cooking range. He didn't hear the flap of the screen door nor the thump of Bohannon's old boots on the planks. The battered portable radio on the counter beside him was too loud. Mostly what radios brought up here in these canyons was static mixed with a few faint strains of music. Country western? Bohannon walked over and switched the radio off.

Stubbs, turning over golden slabs of fried mush, gave him a startled look, white cottony eyebrows raised over round china blue eyes. He was in his seventies, a one-time rodeo rider, crippled up now from too many broken bones, and from arthritis in wet weather. But he did more around the stables than most men half his age could do, and cooked besides—though it sometimes pained Bohannon so much watching him limp and wince that Bohannon pretended he preferred his own cooking to the old man's. It was a wry, running joke between them.

"You shouldn't be so quick to switch off radios," Stubbs said. "You might learn stuff to your advantage."

"Is that right?" Bohannon stretched a long arm around Stubbs's stocky form to snag a tall blue and white specked country coffee pot off its burner. He tilted coffee into a thick mug, set the pot back, started off with the mug. "Such as?"

"Such as, the Coast Guard found the *Abalone Queen* just after sundown, adrift twenty miles out." Stubbs took eggs from a big, old refrigerator, slammed the door. Bohannon drew out a chair at the big, round deal eating table in the middle of the kitchen, and sat down. Stubbs laid the six eggs carefully on the counter. "Adrift, because Brick Lightner was passed out drunk. His boy was trying to get at the engine, because the starter wouldn't work. But he wasn't strong enough to pry up the trapdoor. He's only ten, or something like that."

"Ten would be about right." Bohannon was wondering whether he shouldn't shower before breakfast. "So they rescued them both, and Brick is in jail again, right? For killing the otter?"

"You'd think so." Stubbs lifted a black iron skillet and turned over sausages that sizzled. He set the pan back down with a clack. "But they had to let him go." Stubbs turned from the stove and blinked at Bohannon with a little smile. "That surprises you, now, don't it? You know why they had to let him go?"

"I guess you're going to tell me," Bohannon said, and pretended indifference, lighting a cigarette, tasting the coffee. It was too hot. He burned his mouth. "I guess that radio is a cornucopia."

"It's a Sony," Stubbs said, "but it talks English. He had the wrong gun, that's why. It was a deer rifle killed that otter. Like you said last night. But the gun Brick Lightner had on board his boat—it was a shotgun."

"I'll be damned," Bohannon said mildly.

"And there's more," Stubbs said.

Bohannon gave his head a shake. "I don't know how much more I can stand. Didn't Lucille press charges for Brick snatching Nolan? She and her husband got court orders against him for that."

"Didn't say nothing on the radio about that

part," Stubbs said again. "See? I told you it was no cornucopia."

"Just a simple Sony," Bohannon said. "What more?"

"Brick Lightner wasn't back at his place more than a few hours, and somebody come in and shot him dead."

Bohannon stared. "Who? What for?"

"There, now." Satisfied, Stubbs turned back to his cooking. "I got you good, didn't I? I says you ought to listen to the radio."

"Who was it?" Bohannon said.

And a voice said, "They want it to be me."

Bohannon turned. The voice came in from the long, covered plank walk that fronted the house, came in through the open door and windows of the kitchen. It was a fine, fresh morning, nippy but sunny and blue-skied. Sage and eucalyptus perfumed the breeze. Bohannon thought he knew the voice. The silhouette at the screen door made him sure of it. It was Sharon Webb's, chunky and hippy and stalwart. He went and opened the screen door.

"Come in," he said. "They bound you over?"

"I drove to the sheriff like a bat out of hell to report a murder," she said, "and next thing I know I'm being booked and fingerprinted. Said the gun in my pickup had been fired. Nobody's fingerprints on it but mine. I'm out on bail because Ford Larrimore"—she meant the judge—"is a dear old friend. And I pay my taxes."

"Have some coffee?" Bohannon said.

"Breakfast, Miz Webb?" Stubbs said.

"I'm too angry to eat," she told him, "thank you." She said to Bohannon, "But, yes, I'll drink some coffee."

"How did you happen to find him?" Bohannon asked this after they sat down at the table together. "Was he dead when you got there?"

"No way." She gave her cropped gray head a shake. "He was alive and ornery as ever, and I was giving him a large piece of my mind over shooting that otter."

"How did you know he'd come home?" Bohannon said.

"I guess you can't get TV up here, can you?" she said.

"Not even cable," he said. "Was it on the news?"

"At eleven. That they'd towed the *Abalone Queen* in, and weren't holding Brick in the killing of the otter."

"Because he had the wrong kind of gun," Bohannon said.

"Fiddle-faddle," Sharon Webb said. "Why hadn't he stashed his 30-30 aboard the boat earlier, days ago? Why didn't he throw it overboard after he shot the otter?" She gulped coffee and set the mug down loudly. "Of course, Brick Lightner killed that otter. You heard him say he was going to. Who else would, anyway? For what reason?"

Bohannon shrugged. "So now it's your gun that's in question. Somebody used it to kill him while you were in the kitchen, talking to him? Is that how it was?"

"Bullet went spang into his back while we stood there talking." Bohannon's cigarette pack lay on the bleached white surface of the table. She reached for it with stubby, shaking fingers, pulled a cigarette from it, set the cigarette in her mouth. "I shouldn't do this. Poisoning myself, poisoning the atmosphere. But I keep seeing the look on his face when the bullet hit. Like the devil had grabbed him. He wasn't surprised—he was plain terrified." Bohannon used a thumbnail on a wooden match, and held the flame for her. The cigarette smoked. She inhaled the smoke, and closed her eyes for a moment gratefully. She let the smoke out through her snub nose, opened her eyes, and looked into Bohannon's face. "I need your help. Everyone knows how I hated him. It's as natural for the sheriff, the county attorney, any jury to decide I killed him as it was for me to decide he killed that otter. Which he did, damn it."

"I'll see what I can do," Bohannon said.

The Lightner place was not yet an eyesore, but it was getting there. Yellowing white paint peeled from the clapboards, window screens were torn and curling, and trickles of rust had run down from the corners of the window sills. The composition shingle roof showed seams of graying tar at leakage points. Weeds sprouted through the crushed abalone shell that paved the ground. Beside the house, a dory tilted on blocks, half scraped of its paint, a job begun and abandoned long ago. A strip of shiplap had sprung loose from the warp of rain and sun. Bohannon rolled his dusty pickup past, looking at the neighborhood. The houses were small, old, and because of the humpiness of the foothill terrain, scattered. The nearest place on Lightner's side of the patchy roadway was downhill and cut off by a stand of brushy trees. The house in sight across the road was steeply downhill, too. They wouldn't have seen anything that happened at Lightner's from there. But by craning his neck, he caught a glimpse of blue paint up the slope. He took a wrong turning, and got lost for five minutes. Then he found the road.

The blue paint was on window frames and the door of a place made out of native stone. Eccentric. A fairy tale cottage. Rocks in terraces made a garden in front, with too many plaster elves and iron deer and flamingos. There was also an ugly precast cement fountain. Bohannon climbed in his worn boots between these frights and rapped the door that was arched at the top. He expected a gnome to open it. But it was an old man, bare-chested, grizzled, muscular, leathery. Of course. Carl Tunis. Crazy Carl. It had been years since Bohannon had called him to mind. His lunatic letters used to appear in the paper all the time. If Bohannon had been asked, he'd have said Tunis was dead.

He wore grimy brown walking shorts and sweaty sandals. He had a handful of prunes, and kept popping these into his mouth and chewing them with false teeth that rattled like castinets. He held the hand out to Bohannon. "Have a prune, Sheriff. I'm eighty-three years old, and I do a hundred pushups a day. You're breathing hard. From those steps. I can run up those steps top speed and never notice. I'm healthy because I eat only dried fruits, raw vegetables, and nuts."

"No, thanks," Bohannon said. "Did you see or hear anything down at the Lightner place last night?"

"I go to bed with the chickens," Carl Tunis said. "It's the law of nature. Man's an animal, just like a horse or a cow. They go to bed when the sun goes down."

"Last night—the shot that killed Brick Lightner didn't wake you up?"

"Matter of fact, what woke me up was all the cars," Tunis said. "A person doesn't live in Madrone to sleep in the middle of roaring traffic. A person expects quiet up here at night. I got up and looked out. Good moon, last night. Lightner's looked like a parking lot." Tunis blew a prune pit past Bohannon's ear, and clapped a hand to his mouth to keep his teeth from flying after it.

"You recognize any of the cars?" Bohannon said.

"Shiny big one, looked expensive, European, I think. Lightner's red pickup, of course. That Webb woman's ditsy little Jap pickup. And a pale color van. Four."

"Did you see any of the drivers?" Bohannon said.

"Shadowy," Tunis said. "The gun went off. I seen the fire from the barrel. Outside in the back. Heard glass break, too. Window glass, it was, I guess, from the radio."

"Which car drove off first?" Bohannon said.

"Fancy new one. Tall man got in it. I don't know him. It's too far. Turn yourself around and look down there. You can see how far it is. And Brick Lightner, he doesn't trim the trees, does he? Hard to do that from inside a bottle." The old man cackled at his joke. Bohannon turned as ordered, and had to agree it was hard to see. Tunis said, "He wore spectacles, though. You know, a man wouldn't have to do that if he'd eat raw carrots every day. People go against nature. It's what kills them. I'm going to live forever." He pounded his barrel chest with his fists, stood straight, drew air in noisily, exhaled it. The loose false teeth glared white in the morning sun. "It's a wonderful thing, the gift of life. People shouldn't mistreat it."

"Did you see Sharon Webb leave?" Bohannon said.

"That woman is a meddler," Tunis said. "Can't leave things alone to take their natural course. If you're a meddler, you're going to meddle once too often. I've got nothing against a person playing a tune. It's when they expect everybody else to dance to it, the trouble begins. Yes, I saw her leave, slam out through the kitchen door in a panic. He wouldn't dance to her tune, now, would he—Brick? And she got fed up with it, and killed him. People will drive you crazy if you let them." He wagged his head of dirty white locks. "Trick is to breathe deep, control your heartbeat, stay serene."

"Who did the van belong to?" Bohannon said.

"Beats me," Tunis said. "Nobody from around here."

Bohannon wanted Gerard with him now, but when he rang the sheriff station from the pay phone by the new 76 station on the highway, Gerard was out in a patrol car someplace up a canyon on business involving stolen cattle. Bohannon frowned at the glittery steel pushbuttons of the phone and chewed his lip. He could ask for uniforms to back him up. If he was sure. He wasn't sure. Not a hundred percent. At last he mumbled thanks and hung up.

Householders were out walking expensive dogs up and down the steep, crooked trails of Settlers Cove. New houses were being built all over, which meant the pines were thinning out. But there were still enough of them to keep the roads in chilly shadow this early in the day. He left the pickup at the foot of the zig zag wooden stairs, behind a dark red Mercedes, on whose glossy finish pine needles pattered. Lucille Dodson owned a VW Rabbit. He scuffed with a boot at the little tire imprints in the packed roadside earth where she parked it. He read his watch. She must be taking Nolan to school.

The sliding glass door from the front deck was open again. He could see straight through the house to a rear deck built around the trunks of three big pines. Out there a tall man sat on a bench, sections of the morning paper open on his knees, sections at his feet on the rough redwood planks of the deck. He had a mug of coffee with him, but he wasn't drinking from it. He wasn't reading, either. He was looking away into the woods. Through horn-rimmed spectacles with big round lenses.

"Eliot Dodson?" Bohannon called.

The man's gray-haired head jerked around. He stood up, the papers sliding off his lap. He peered through the shadowy rooms of the house at Bohannon standing out here in pine-needle-splintered sunshine. "Who are you?"

"Bohannon, private investigator. May I come in?"

Dodson came into the house, rounded a dining table, stepped down into the living room. "Why should you?"

"Sharon Webb has been arrested for the murder of Brick Lightner last night, and she's asked me to make inquiries for her. Says she didn't do it." The man had come no nearer. Bohannon still had to raise his voice. It was quiet in these woods. It didn't seem right to him for everybody with ears to hear him. He stepped indoors. "A witness saw you at the Lightner house around midnight. I thought you could tell me what happened there."

"What witness?" Dodson said.

"A neighbor. He saw your car. He heard the shot, the breaking window, saw you run to your car and drive off."

"It was dark," Dodson said. "It wasn't me."

"There was a bright moon," Bohannon said. "He had your description right. He described the car."

"I'm calling my lawyer." Dodson took steps.

"What for? You're not being accused of anything. All I need is a witness. Witnesses don't need lawyers. Suspects need lawyers. Am I supposed to suspect you of a crime? You surprise me."

Dodson looked uncertain. "What do you want to know?"

"Sharon Webb claims she was in Lightner's kitchen, talking to him, when he was shot. My witness says he saw her come out the back door, but that doesn't prove she was inside when the shot was fired. Was she?"

Dodson's thin mouth worked. He sat down on a long couch, picked up a phone off an end table, but he didn't push any buttons. He set the phone back. He sighed. "All right. When I got home here from San Francisco, and learned what he'd done to Nolan, I drove over there, yes."

"Had he hurt him?" Bohannon said.

"Not hurt in the common meaning, no. But he'd rousted him out of a sound sleep, dragged him off to sea in the dark, passed out drunk. The boat was drifting, the boy couldn't start the engine. He couldn't get to it under the planks. It was terrifying. The child was a wreck."

"And you were going to do what to Lightner?"

"I was— I was—" Dodson's long, pale face grew red. "Ah, hell. I was furious. I don't know what I was going to do. There's a court order forbidding Brick to touch the boy. I'm trying— I'm trying to be a decent father to him, a proper role model. And that grungy drunk—"

"I know how you feel," Bohannon said. "Did you hear them talking? Did you look through the kitchen window? You're tall enough."

Dodson eyed him sourly, reached for the telephone again, didn't pick it up. He drew a deep breath. "Yes," he said, "I did. She was in there. Yelling at him about killing that otter. He had a bottle in his hand, and kept swigging from it, and grinning at her, mocking her. You know what he thought of women. Then the gun went off. He pitched forward on his face. I'll never forget it."

"And you ran like hell," Bohannon said.

"So would you. Everyone knew I hated him. Twenty people can step forward and testify they've heard me say I'd like to kill him. I never meant it."

"Did you say it last night?" Bohannon asked. "Where anybody heard you?"

Dodson looked sick. "We called Dr. Hesseltine to give Nolan a shot so he could sleep. The poor kid was shattered." Dodson eyed Bohannon gloomily. "The doctor heard me, loud and clear. You know Belle. Tough old dame. She said I was the one who needed the shot. I roared on out of here. I wanted my hands around that bastard's throat."

"Brick could take you out, drunk or sober."

"I wasn't thinking," Dodson said.

"The ride over there didn't cool you off? You didn't realize you couldn't brace him with your bare hands? You didn't see the rifle in Sharon Webb's pickup and—"

"No." Dodson stood up sharply. "Absolutely not. It wasn't me. There was someone else there. I heard them moving around, back of the house, brush crackling."

"But you didn't see who it was?"

"There wasn't time. The gun went off, and I knew if I was caught there, I'd be blamed."

"There was a light-colored van there," Bohannon said. "Maybe the shooter came in that."

"I saw it, but I don't know who owns it."

Bohannon made a face. "Nobody knows." He sighed. "Come on, Mr. Dodson. Let's go over to the sheriff's, and get your story on record."

"And set your client free," Dodson said.

Bohannon blinked. "You have something against her?"

"Not a thing." Dodson sat, picked up the phone, punched a number. "But if she didn't do it, won't they put me in her place?" He broke off to speak a man's name into the phone. He listened, grimaced, grunted "Damn," and slammed down the receiver. For a moment, he slumped back on the couch, eyes shut, mouth a line of disgust. Then he sat up, blew air out noisily, ran fingers through his hair, and looked at Bohannon. "Lawyer's not available. My old buddy. Europe. Three weeks. I'm in for it now, right?"

"Only Sharon Webb's fingerprints are on that rifle."

Dodson grunted. "But I was wearing gloves,

wasn't I? It's an ingrained habit, since I bought the Mercedes. Body oils discolor the leather on the steering wheel."

Bohannon shrugged. "If it comes to that, the county will furnish you a lawyer. But it won't come to that."

Dodson stood up. "Just let me use the bathroom."

He didn't come back from the bathroom. When, after a long minute, Bohannon called out his name and went looking for him, the bathroom window stood open. Down below, the Mercedes's diesel engine rattled to life. Bohannon ran through the house to the deck in time to see the broad, shiny car roll off down the trail.

When he reached the foot of the zig zag stairs among the fern and poison oak and the chilly shadows of the pines he heard a car coming. It rounded the bend above, and it was Lucille Dodson's white Rabbit with the black cloth top. She parked in those four little dents the wheels had made in the road edge and got out, looking puzzled to find him here. She brought a shoulder bag out of the car, let the door fall shut, and came up to him. Quizzical.

"Where's Eliot?"

"You tell me," Bohannon said, and outlined for her what had happened. "Where would he go to hide?"

"He has no reason to hide." She looked along the road as if she expected him to come driving back up it right now. As if maybe he'd gone out for a newspaper or cigarettes. "He didn't kill Brick Lightner.

He couldn't. He's the gentlest man in the world."
Gazing up at him, her face like some badly bruised flower, her eyes filled with tears. "He's not capable of violence, Mr. Bohannon."

"He admitted he was in a rage last night," Bohannon said. "Over what Brick had put Nolan through."

"Nolan's all right," she said. "He's just fine this morning. As if nothing had happened."

"But last night he was so shaken up you had to phone Belle Hesseltine to quiet him down. And Eliot says Belle heard him say he was going to kill Brick."

"Words," Lucille scoffed. "He was upset. Surely Belle understood that. She's a very wise old woman."

"He went there, just the same," Bohannon said. "And Brick Lightner was killed. So maybe it wasn't just words."

"Excuse me." She brushed past him, and started up the stairs, quickly, angrily.

"You going to phone him?" Bohannon called.

She stopped, turned back. "I don't know where."

"He shouldn't have run," Bohannon said. "It makes him look guilty as hell. If he calls, tell him to go to the sheriff and tell him what he told me."

"To help you earn your pay?" Lucille turned, climbed a few steps, turned back again. "Do you know the real irony of all this? I mean—if the Webb woman did kill Brick?"

"Tell me the real irony," Bohannon said.

"Brick didn't shoot the otter," she said.

"Not with that shotgun," Bohannon said, "but—"
She shook her head. "Not with any gun. Nolan

told me on the way to school just now. Brick heated a can of chili for Nolan's breakfast, then passed out on his bunk. All he did all day was sleep, drink, sleep. With Nolan at the helm. He steered strictly away from the kelp beds. And Brick never once picked up a gun."

"A dark red late model Mercedes complete with license number," Gerard said. "It won't be hard to spot. We'll have him soon." He smiled wryly at Bohannon across his paperwork-strewn desk. "You've done it again, Hack. There'll be formalities, Miz Webb. But as far as the sheriff's department is concerned, you're in the clear."

The stocky little woman gave him a grudging smile for a moment, then looked grieved. "That poor little boy—he never seems to end up in the right place. And as for Lucille, why is it some women are so wretchedly unlucky."

"She doesn't have a gift for picking husbands," Gerard said. "That's for sure."

Bohannon made a face. "I don't know. She calls Dodson gentle. And she ought to know the difference. I wish I was as sure as you that he did it."

"Gloves smeared the prints on Miz Webb's rifle," Gerard said, "in just the places where prints would be when someone held it to fire it. And he admitted to you he wore gloves."

"He also said somebody else was there," Bohannon said. "Out in back of the house in the dark."

"Maybe Brick had some woman there and sent her outside when Miz Webb here showed up. Or she went outside on her own, so as not to be seen with Brick. Who would want to?"

214

"The owner of the white van," Bohannon said. "Sharon here saw it, too." The little woman nodded her cropped gray head. "That makes three witnesses now. You know of any woman of the type that would go with Brick Lightner who drives a white van? Or why he'd let some pickup from a tavern drive herself to his place?"

Gerard snorted. "Makes it too easy to leave."

"And when she got a look at that house inside," Sharon Webb said, "she'd want to leave. It's filthy."

"If it was the killer," Gerard said, "we need a motive. We know both Miz Webb and Eliot Dodson had it in for Brick, and why." He raised eyebrows at Bohannon. "Who else, Hack?"

Bohannon stared at him for a minute, then stood up. "You want to drive Sharon home?" he asked Gerard. "I just remembered something." He left the office at a run.

He rapped the aluminum screen door through which he could smell cooking. The sea breeze blew on his back. The sun glared off the fresh white paint on the stucco of the back of the building. A fat Mexican woman in an expanse of chili-smeared apron came and pushed open the door. He held out the picnic basket to her. "Thank *señora* Hawes for this," he said. "The plates and tablecloth and glasses are inside." She smiled with marvelous teeth, and dimples showed in her terra-cotta cheeks. She nodded, and reached for the basket.

"I will tell her, *señor*," she said.

"And say I'm sorry I missed her," he said. "The meal was delicious. Did you cook it?"

The plump shoulders moved in girlish embarrassment and pleasure. "*Si*, but the recipes, they are Meeses Hawes's."

"Where is she, today?" Bohannon said.

"You know her daughters? In Lompoc. The one who was just married a few months ago. And now she and her young husband, they have found a house. They wanted Meeses Hawes to come look at it and see whether it is right for them." The fat woman craned back to look at something. "She ought to be returning soon." The smile came back. "Thank you for the basket, *señor*."

"Thank you," he said, turned away, turned back. "Tell me. The other morning, the morning when Mrs. Hawes packed that basket for us—you remember?"

"*Si, señor*." She nodded.

"A truck delivered bread to you from San Francisco," he said. "Is that right? Were you here to receive it?"

"Meeses Hawes," the woman said, "she live upstairs." She stepped out and pointed to a flight of steps that climbed to rooms over the restaurant. "They come with the bread very early. I am not yet here. Meeses Hawes meets them and takes the bread inside here to put in warming ovens." A shadow of misgiving crossed the round face. The woman cocked her head at him. "But that morning, when I arrived, the bread was stacked outside here, on this step."

"Mrs. Hawes wasn't here to receive it?" Bohannon said.

"She came late that morning," the woman said. "I remember. How did you know, *señor*?"

"Not from upstairs," he said. "She came in her car, isn't that right? Where from, do you know?"

"*Si*, it is as you say," the woman said. "But no, I do not know from where." A timer bell rang behind the woman in the kitchen. She gave a start and pulled the screen door shut. "You must excuse me, now. *Señor*. The cooking."

"Thank you," Bohannon said. He turned away, and the wind took his hat. He grabbed for it, missed, it hit the sandy earth and rolled along at the base of the wall. The wind was brisk, he lunged after the hat, it reached the corner of the building and disappeared. He rounded the building corner, and grabbed for the hat and sprawled. He was climbing to his feet, slapping the grit off his clothes with the hat, when a white van swung in to park beside the building. The driver was Dorothy Hawes. She saw him through the windshield, gave him a wave of her hand, and climbed down out of the van. Her smile was half wince against the brightness of the sun and the stiffness of the breeze.

"Why, Hack, how nice to see you again."

Bohannon went to her, and kicked the left front tire of the van. He said to her, "I guess not," and squatted, and from in front of the tire gathered up what his scuffed boot had knocked loose. He rose and held it out in his hand for her to look at. "You know what that is?"

"Kind of shiny." She was mystified. "Like seashell."

"Abalone shell," Bohannon said. "And there's only one place around here that's got a yard full of that anymore. Brick Lightner's." He walked a-round the truck now, stooping, digging with his clasp knife at the treads of the other tires. "This van was parked there the night Brick was shot. Three people saw it." He folded the blade into the

217

knife and dropped the knife into the frayed pocket of his jeans. "Why did you do it, Dorothy? First kill the otter, and then—"

"Because they let him go," she cried. "That was all I meant to do. I never meant to take a human life. I'm not like him. I'm not, Hack. You must believe that. He killed my husband. He killed Bob, as sure as sure can be. You know that's true. And the court blamed the storm and let him off. Let him off scott free to drink and bully his life away."

"Easy, Dorothy." Bohannon put hands on her shoulders to try to calm her. She shook him off.

"I'm not like that. I thought if I killed the otter, he'd get his punishment at last. Then I saw on the TV news he had the wrong kind of gun and they had to let him go, and that's how it would always be, wouldn't it? The law would never get him. I told you the other morning, there is no justice. And you know that, Hack."

"No justice in murder," Bohannon said.

"I only went there to"—she wrung her hands, looked at the sky, turned with a jerk to look at the sea, tears streaming down her face—"I don't know, to tell him to his ugly face the awful thing he'd done to me, drowning my Bob, the lonely, drudging life he'd sentenced me to."

"And just by luck you saw the rifle in Sharon Webb's pickup? And there was a clear shot through the kitchen window, right between Brick's shoulder blades, and you decided there was justice, after all? And you were the instrument?" He stepped around the van, yanked open the door, climbed in, jerked open the glove box, found what he expected, got out of the truck. She was watching him. He held up a pair of driving gloves. "I guess not. You took your own rifle, didn't you? But if you used Sharon Webb's and left it there, it would point suspicion completely away from you, right?"

"I didn't mean to get her into trouble," Dorothy Hawes wailed. "I'd have come forward to take the blame, Hack. Truly, I would. You see, both my girls are grown and married and secure now. Now I could do what I'd waited all these years"—she put her hands to her mouth and gave her head a frightened shake, her eyes wide, watching him. "No. I didn't mean that."

"You came back to kill him," Bohannon said. He jerked his head at the restaurant. "This was only a cover. You came back to kill Brick Lightner, and that was all you came back for." She seemed to lose starch all of a sudden. The tears that ran were tears of exhaustion. She swayed, and he stepped over to hold her up. "Come on," he said gently. "It's all over now." He led her toward his battered truck, helped her up into it, slammed the door. When he climbed in on the driver's side, she was slumped over against the door, cheek pressed to the dusty glass, gazing at the sea, if she was gazing at anything at all. He started the engine, let the brake go, turned the wheel. "You shot the otter, so you do own a rifle. Where is it?"

"I felt so sickened." Her voice was toneless with misery. "I hated myself for killing a helpless creature."

He wheeled the truck out onto the highway.

"I never wanted to kill anything again," she said.

"Nothing helpless, anyway," Bohannon said.

"The rifle's in the restaurant. Behind the counter, under the cash register." She was silent for a while, as the truck rattled towards town. Then she said coldly, "He deserved to die," and that was all she said.

He drove the crooked two-lane blacktop road over the mountains slowly, shifting down a lot. A horse trailer swung along behind the pickup this morning, and its passenger was a gangly weanling who had never been trailered before. Rivera had rigged the trailer with a rail to hold him steady, but careful driving was needed all the same, no sharp turns, no abrupt stops and starts. It grew tiring. His muscles ached with tension and he sweated.

The tall, rambling old house, with its white jigsaw-work verandahs stood quiet among the spring-green foothills. The windows reflected clear blue sky. When they got out of the truck into the still-ness, a freshening breeze cooled him. He unbolted the trailer door and let it down to serve as a ramp. Talking softly, he stepped up into the trailer, and stood a while, stroking the colt's copper-color coat. He took a handful of grain from a pocket and let the soft mouth of the colt lip it from his hand.

He unhitched the youngster and by the halter turned him around and led him down the ramp. His coat glowed in the sunshine. T. Hodges smiled. "Isn't he lovely?" she said. But Bohannon heard the closing of a door, and looked toward the mansion. He had phoned ahead for approval of his plan. And there was Linda on the porch, a nurse with her. He took the halter and began walking the colt up the long lawn past the flowerbeds.

Linda didn't move. Maybe she was daunted by the outdoors, all that sunlit space in front of her. But as he neared the house, the colt nodding obediently beside him, he thought she was watching. Not something dark and horrible in the past, but what was happening here and now. Then he was close enough to be sure her gaze was on the beautiful young animal who, when Bohannon paused, did a little quick-stepping on his knobby legs.

"Linda?" Bohannon called. "Come see the colt."

She hesitated. She glanced at the nurse. The nurse smiled and nodded. Linda moved, stepped out, not quickly, almost as if walking were a new sensation. She reached the top of the long steps and halted. Worry flickered in her face for a moment, then passed, and she came down the steps. Slowly at first, then more quickly. She circled the neck of the little horse with her arms, and rubbed her cheek against his smooth coat. Her eyes shone. Then she saw T. Hodges, and smiled.

"Hello," she said. "I'm Linda Bohannon."

FOR THE BEST IN PAPERBACKS, LOOK FOR THE

In every corner of the world, on every subject under the sun, Penguin represents quality and variety—the very best in publishing today.

For complete information about books available from Penguin—including Pelicans, Puffins, Peregrines, and Penguin Classics—and how to order them, write to us at the appropriate address below. Please note that for copyright reasons the selection of books varies from country to country.

In the United Kingdom: For a complete list of books available from Penguin in the U.K., please write to *Dept E.P., Penguin Books Ltd, Harmondsworth, Middlesex, UB7 0DA.*

In the United States: For a complete list of books available from Penguin in the U.S., please write to *Dept BA, Penguin,* Box 999, Bergenfield, New Jersey 07621-0999.

In Canada: For a complete list of books available from Penguin in Canada, please write to *Penguin Books Canada Ltd, 2801 John Street, Markham, Ontario L3R 1B4.*

In Australia: For a complete list of books available from Penguin in Australia, please write to the *Marketing Department, Penguin Books Australia Ltd, P.O. Box 257, Ringwood, Victoria 3134.*

In New Zealand: For a complete list of books available from Penguin in New Zealand, please write to the *Marketing Department, Penguin Books (NZ) Ltd, Private Bag, Takapuna, Auckland 9.*

In India: For a complete list of books available from Penguin, please write to *Penguin Overseas Ltd, 706 Eros Apartments, 56 Nehru Place, New Delhi, 110019.*

In Holland: For a complete list of books available from Penguin in Holland, please write to *Penguin Books Nederland B.V., Postbus 195, NL–1380AD Weesp, Netherlands.*

In Germany: For a complete list of books available from Penguin, please write to *Penguin Books Ltd, Friedrichstrasse 10–12, D–6000 Frankfurt Main 1, Federal Republic of Germany.*

In Spain: For a complete list of books available from Penguin in Spain, please write to *Longman Penguin España, Calle San Nicolas 15, E–28013 Madrid, Spain.*

In Japan: For a complete list of books available from Penguin in Japan, please write to *Longman Penguin Japan Co Ltd, Yamaguchi Building, 2-12-9 Kanda Jimbocho, Chiyuoda-Ku, Tokyo 101, Japan.*

☐ MURDOCK FOR HIRE
Robert Ray

When he is hired to find a dead man's missing antique coin collection, private detective Matt Murdock discovers an international crime ring that is much more than a nickle-and-dime operation.

256 pages   *ISBN: 0-14-010679-0*   **$3.95**

☐ BRIARPATCH
Ross Thomas

This Edgar Award-winning thriller is the story of Benjamin Dill, who returns to the Sunbelt city of his youth to attend his sister's funeral—and find her killer.

384 pages   *ISBN: 0-14-010581-6*   **$3.95**

☐ DEATH'S SAVAGE PASSION
Orania Papazoglou

Suspense is killing Romance, and the Romance Writers of America are outraged. When a fresh, enthusiastic creator of the loathed hybrid, Romantic Suspense, arrives on the scene, someone shows her just how murderous competition can be.   *180 pages*   *ISBN: 0-14-009967-0*   **$3.50**

☐ GOLD BY GEMINI
Jonathan Gash

Lovejoy, the antiques dealer whom the *Chicago Sun-Times* calls "one of the most likable rogues in mystery history," searches for Roman gold coins and greedy bird-killers on the Isle of Man.

224 pages   *ISBN: 0-451-82185-8*   **$3.95**

☐ REILLY: ACE OF SPIES
Robin Bruce Lockhart

This is the incredible true story of superspy Sidney Reilly, said to be the inspiration for James Bond. Robin Bruce Lockhart's book tells the thrilling story of the British Secret Service agent's shadowy Russian past and near-legendary exploits in espionage and in love.

192 pages   *ISBN: 0-14-006895-3*   **$4.95**

☐ STRANGERS ON A TRAIN
Patricia Highsmith

Almost against his will, Guy Haines is trapped in a nightmare of shared guilt when he agrees to kill the father of the man who will kill Guy's wife. The basis for the unforgettable Hitchcock thriller.

256 pages   *ISBN: 0-14-003796-9*   **$4.95**

☐ THE THIN WOMAN
Dorothy Cannell

An interior designer who is also a passionate eater, her rented companion who writes trashy novels, and a rich dead uncle with a conditional will are the principals in this delicious thriller.   *242 pages*   *ISBN: 0-14-007947-5*   **$3.95**

FOR THE BEST IN MYSTERY, LOOK FOR THE

☐ **SMALLBONE DECEASED**
Michael Gilbert

Henry Bohun had joined the law firm to work on insurance cases not murders
. . . until one of the firm's trustees, Marcus Smallbone, turned up dead in a deed
box.   *208 pages   ISBN: 0-14-011077-1*   **$3.95**

☐ **POST-MORTEM EFFECTS**
Thomas Boyle

Supercop Francis DeSales must find the madman behind a wave of violent crimes
that has rocked the ethnic neighborhoods of Brooklyn—before the whole city
blows apart.   *288 pages   ISBN: 0-14-009753-8*   **$3.95**

☐ **SARATOGA LONGSHOT**
Stephen Dobyns

Tracking down Sam, the son of an old flame, Charlie Bradshaw winds up in New
York, where Sam is involved in a big-time drug deal and Charlie's presence is
decidedly unwanted by both the boy and the New York cop who is investigating
the case.   *248 pages   ISBN: 0-14-009627-2*   **$3.95**

☐ **A DIME TO DANCE BY**
Walter Walker

When young lawyer Chuckie Bishop defends a cop who has killed an unarmed
burglar in Chuckie's blue-collar hometown, he discovers a web of political, financial, and sexual intrigue that threatens to destroy his dreams forever.
                      380 pages   ISBN: 0-14-007347-7   **$3.95**

FOR THE BEST IN MYSTERY, LOOK FOR THE

☐ **CAROLINE MINUSCULE**
Andrew Taylor

Glittering diamonds and a medieval script prove a lethal combination when a
leading authority on the Caroline Minuscule style of script is murdered.
234 pages   ISBN: 0-14-007099-0   **$3.95**

☐ **THE PENGUIN COMPLETE FATHER BROWN**
G.K. Chesterton

Here, in one volume, are forty-nine sensational cases investigated by the high
priest of detective fiction, Father Brown, whose cherubic face and unworldly
simplicity disguise an uncanny understanding of the criminal mind.
718 pages   ISBN: 0-14-009766-X   **$9.95**

☐ **APPLEBY AND THE OSPREYS**
Michael Innes

When Lord Osprey is murdered in Clusters, his ancestral home, with an Oriental
dagger, it falls to Sir John Appleby and Lord Osprey's faithful butler, Bagot, to
pick out the clever killer from an assortment of the lord's eccentric house
guests.   184 pages   ISBN: 0-14-011092-5   **$3.95**

☐ **THE BODY IN THE BILLIARD ROOM**
H.R.F. Keating

The great detective and lovable bumbler Inspector Ghote is summoned from
Bombay to the oh-so-English Ooty Club to discover why there is a dead man on
the very billiard table where snooker was invented.
256 pages   ISBN: 0-14-010171-3   **$3.95**

☐ **STEPS GOING DOWN**
Joseph Hansen

Frail old Stewart Moody is found one morning strangled with the oxygen tube that
was keeping him alive, in this powerful tale of obsessive love and the tawdry
emptiness of evil.   320 pages   ISBN: 0-14-008810-5   **$3.50**